NATHAN SELLYN

INDIGENOUS BEASTS

RAINCOAST BOOKS

Vancouver

Raincoast Books gratefully acknowledges the ongoing support of the Canada
Council for the Arts, the British Columbia Arts Council and
the Government of Canada through the Book Publishing Industry
Development Program (BPIDP).

Edited by Martha Sharpe
Interior design by Teresa Bubela
Cover artwork and design by Jason Munn (thesmallstakes.com)
Author photo by Rob Masefield

Library and Archives Canada Cataloguing in Publication
Sellyn, Nathan, 1982-
        Indigenous beasts / Nathan Sellyn.

ISBN 10 1-55192-927-9
ISBN 13 978-1-55192-927-9

        I. Title.
PS8637.E485I54 2006   C813'.6   C2005-905750-5

Raincoast Books
9050 Shaughnessy Street
Vancouver, British Columbia
Canada V6P 6E5
www.raincoast.com

Raincoast Books is committed to protecting the environment and to the
responsible use of natural resources. We are working with suppliers and
printers to phase out our use of paper produced from ancient forests. This
book is printed with vegetable-based inks on 100% ancient-forest-free paper,
processed chlorine- and acid-free. For further information, visit our website
at www.raincoast.com/publishing.

Printed in Canada by Friesens.

10 9 8 7 6 5 4 3 2 1

To Millie and Wolfie,
for all the stories I never had the chance to hear.

INDIGENOUS BEASTS

CLEANING UP

MICHEL'S DOORMAN, Albert, had us sign our names, then read them aloud to us.

"Trevor Huffs and ... Benito Mussolineye?"

"That's Moo-so-lee-nee," Danny said. "It's Italian."

Albert was an old guy; his oversized Semitic features and bald head made him look like one of the suspects from *Clue*. And he hated us. Hated. Under his dark blue jacket and polished brass buttons, old Al fucking hated us. Not because we posed any threat to Michel upstairs, or to the building's other, more sophisticated tenants. Albert hated us because he knew Danny was fucking with him, using these ridiculous names, and that even if he did something about it, even if he asked for some ID and made Michel come down to approve everything, we would still get in and go up. In that apartment building and in the world, we had Albert beat. We had him beat and he knew it.

He nodded to Danny.

"Floor thirty, gentlemen," he said, looking down. "Have a good night."

"Benito Mussolini always enjoys Saturday night," Danny said over his shoulder. "Consider it a promise."

I knew that if I turned, Colonel Mustard would be looking at our backs with narrowed eyes.

It was around eight, it had just gotten dark. The plan was to pick up Mich, hang out for a little, then all cruise out for the evening. A club we liked, Atlantis, was having a black-tie night. It was a little ways off in suburbia, but the girls, thanks to the trophy-wife gene pool, were always incredible.

"Trev," Danny said in the elevator. "You alright?" We ignored the view at our backs and studied ourselves in the mirrored doors. I had on a black tux with a black bow tie and vest, pretty simple stuff. Danny was wearing a tux too, but with a cummerbund. He also had our coke, and Mich's crystal. Drugs were his business, although Mich and I weren't exactly customers. More like friends of the program.

"Yeah, 'course," I said. "Why? Don't I look alright?"

"Nah, yeah, you look fine," Danny said. "Just watching out for you, right?" I nodded and rolled my shoulders. I don't like being worried about.

"Big night," I said as the doors parted.

"Big night." Danny pumped a fist in the air.

The whole building was bankers, twenty-somethings from the top universities, all with the same leased BMWs and short, textured haircuts. Michel was on the thirtieth of thirty-one floors. He had a cinder block keeping the door open, and we walked straight in.

The apartment smelled of bleach. Mich was sprawled out on the couch in a white jacket with black pants and a pink bow tie. He also had an excellent tan. He was watching a video, and the television screen bathed him in ultraviolet.

"Cutlass! Danny boy!" He came over and hugged us both. I don't know why he always called me Cutlass. But it sounded pretty hard, so I never complained. "Sit down, guys, please," he said.

It was a sultan's space, but sparsely furnished. Two swollen leather couches, a club chair, a glass coffee table, and a plasma TV the size of a blackboard. The opposite wall was just windows. The view overlooked downtown Vancouver all the way out to the anthill of East Hastings, North America's AIDS capital.

Mich disappeared and came back with a bottle of Bacardi Solera, three shot glasses, and three bottles of Evian. Normally, when we were doing drugs, we tried to watch the alcohol. When you go to Playland, you take the rides one at a time. But we were all dressed up, and that was a good enough excuse to go a little crazy.

"Renee coming by?" I asked. Michel had been seeing the same girl for a while, almost three months. I liked her, actually. She was shorter than I usually go for, barely five feet, but her body had a very athletic quality that I found attractive. She had been a gymnast, she maybe told me once. Plus she laughed at our jokes, and never got too out of control. Those are valuable qualities in a woman. One thing I can't stand: people who make themselves other people's responsibility. Renee was never that, and too many girls are.

"Think so, don't know," Mich said. "I left her a message."

"Does she know to get dressed up?" Danny hunched forward on the couch, elbows on his knees.

"She better, I left it in the message. Shit, look at that." Mich was watching *Girls Really Gone Wild*. Two naked girls were sprawled out on an animal skin, fighting over a hundred-dollar bill. He always seemed to be watching this, or else the Platinum Edition of *Wall Street*, which he had never seen all the way through, and would unfailingly turn off after the scene where Bud moves to the Upper East Side.

"How can you not appreciate this, am I right?" Michel waved a hand at the screen. The girls' bodies were streaked in dirt and mud, one of them was bleeding. She kicked the other girl in the jaw, then began pulling her hair. They were grunting at each other like they were auditioning for *Nell*.

"No, I think she'll be here," Mich said. "Better be here, you know?" He traced a woman's figure in the air, then humped it.

"Should I wait?" Danny said, gesturing at his pocket.

"No, fuck that. She doesn't need it, she'll do whatever."

"Okay," Danny said.

"Besides, if she's not here at nine, we go without her. I mean, she's a great girl, but there's an agenda for the evening, you know? Boom! Right, Cutlass?"

Danny stood up and went to the washroom.

"Damn straight," I said.

We filled shots and chased them with the water. Onscreen, the bleeding girl secured the cash, and, victorious, began to masturbate in slow motion. The loser crawled submissively to the corner of the frame. Once there, she curled into the fetal position and passed out.

"How's your mum?" I said.

"She is good, she is not bad." Mich and I had grown up on the same block in North Van. My mum ran off with a contractor while I was still breast-feeding, leaving my dad and me to fend for ourselves. Since he often worked late at the office, I needed somewhere to go after school. For a while, it was to a big house two blocks over from the school. Maria, the Spanish woman who lived there watched after me and a half-dozen other kids. She had three poodles, aggressive little grey things with no barks.

Their voice boxes had been cut out. They had wet, raspy coughs, like they were choking on their own stomachs.

Then in fourth grade I started going to Michel's house. His mum didn't work, and he had no brothers or sisters, so she would take care of me until my dad came home. Mich and I grew very close, stayed that way through high school. Lost touch a little when he went away to university, but now that we were both living in Vancouver again it was just like old times. It was while he was gone that I'd started hanging out with Danny.

"Her feet alright?" His mum had been in the day before for ankle surgery.

"Yeah, real good. I haven't seen her yet, but she called here today. Sounds good. She's gonna be laid up for a few weeks, but then, you know, she'll be marching around again. So it went good, I think."

"Nice, nice." I nodded.

"You, Cutlass?" Mich said. "No lady tonight, I see, but other things are well?" This was a fairly pointless conversation. I mean, Wyatt Earp and Doc Holliday didn't talk while they were playing cards. They saved their lines for when the shooting started. Besides, I had been over here a few nights recently, and there was nothing new to share.

"Yeah, things are going good, buddy." I was working in computers then. The dot-com bubble was long gone, popped as soon as I got close enough to breathe on it, but there was still plenty of cash to be made merging technically unsavvy companies onto the information superhighway.

"I'm actually meeting a girl at Atlantis," I lied. "One from work." Michel's features are very thin, almost elfin. Mine are chunkier, like my face was moulded from leftover dough. The first girl I ever slept with had been one of his ex-girlfriends, a girl who fell in love with him and hooked up with me to stay nearby.

"Excellent," he said. "I'm happy to hear it, you know. You deserve a class act, Cutlass." We looked at the screen instead of each other while we talked. I fixed a shot and passed it to him. He reached for the bottle and increased the pour, sending rum over the brim of the tiny glass and into a puddle on the table. We drank in silence for a few more minutes before Danny came back in with a handful of toilet paper.

Without saying anything, Danny put the plastic baggie of crystals on the table and tapped it so that one fell out. Michel scratched his cheek and watched. He looked up, turned down the television, then shut it off. I could see he had been chewing his nails again, an old habit. All were worn down to raw, pink ends. His thumb was bleeding.

I'd been away from crystal for over a year, since I saw Danny putting together a batch — drain cleaner, lighter fluid, a handful of over-the-counter medications, iodine crystals, of course, paint thinner and red phosphorus, which is basically the strike pad on a matchbook. The ingredients had turned Danny off too, but Mich was still a regular.

"Are we going to save all the coke for the club?" Michel asked. I looked at Danny and bit my lip. They were his drugs.

"Yeah, I dunno, it's not a big deal," Danny said. "You want your shit now?"

"Just gimme that one," Michel's cheek was red where he had been scratching.

"Sure," Danny said. He tucked the bag back away and pulled out a vial of coke. Michel leaned over the table and picked up the crystal between his thumb and forefinger. Placing it carefully on one of the sheets, he twisted the paper around the little diamond. Then he popped the entire package in his mouth, took a long sip from his water, swallowed and sat back. He caught me looking at him and winked.

"Big night, Cutlass," he said. He was parachuting, eating the crystal straight. The advantage to ingestion is the length of the high. Michel could be soaring for almost two days if he had a good trip. Problem is, the shit tastes like month-old milk; it'll make you gag every time. Plus, it'll burn you on the way down. But the toilet paper solves those problems, hiding the taste and protecting your throat. Mich got up and went over to the stereo on the far wall. While he was fiddling, Danny pinched two small bumps onto the table.

"We'll hit the bathroom when we get to the club," he said. That was fine by me; I had no desire to be too amped during the ride over. I pulled out a bill and did my bump, then handed it to him so he could do his. I squeezed my eyes shut for a second.

"Listen to this kid," Danny said.

Michel was whispering under his breath as he flicked through stations on the stereo, giving each one a few seconds of play and then switching it. Most of them were Top 40 and hip-hop, a few were straight dance.

Danny poured out two shots and handed me one. I sipped it and watched Michel. He was tapping his foot to some beat we couldn't hear. Suddenly he stepped back and flung out his arms.

"There we go!" he shouted. It was classical music, the heroic sort you hear at the planetarium while you're waiting for a show to start. He came back to the couch and sat down. "Best shit ever," he said. I didn't know whether he meant the drugs or the music. Danny laughed and smacked his knee. I opened my mouth to make a joke, then forgot it.

The music was getting faster, and a beat began to sound behind it. Danny stood up, and he and Mich started dancing.

With themselves more than with each other, throwing their arms over their heads and shuffling their feet around the tiny space between the coffee table and the couches. Mich had some rhythm, but both of them looked more like caricatures of people enjoying themselves, like they were dancing at prom in a high-school movie.

I took off my jacket and shoes and socks so I could lie down on the couch. The leather was cool against my cheek, and I closed my eyes and smiled. I was thirsty. I sat back up. I wanted more water but my bottle was empty, and the effort it would take to go to the kitchen for another seemed daunting. I grabbed Mich's instead, which was still full. Then I stood up.

"There we go, Cutlass!" Michel had his jacket off too, but only to turn it inside out before shrugging it back on. The lining was bright red, it went well with his bow tie. Danny had his head down, but his feet kept pumping. His moves still didn't look good, but they made me want to shake with him. I jumped on the couch and tried to touch the ceiling with my hands. I couldn't reach. Michel started clapping, and Danny climbed onto the couch too. They were dancing better now; we all were, getting smooth to the music. I closed my eyes and jumped.

"Cutlass," Michel yelled, "you happy?"

I gave him a Billy Idol sneer.

"You see that, Danny?" Michel said. "Trev's a happy boy! Look at him!"

I balled my fists and put them by my head, like a boxer. I felt good, really good. My one bump seemed like a dozen, and the leather was soft under my bare feet.

Then Michel tackled me. Not hard. Just jumped over the table and pulled my legs out so I landed on the couch, then started punching me in the shoulders, older-brother style.

He only got in a few shots before Danny was on his back, grabbing his shoulders and pushing him down into me. I reached out and grabbed Danny's thigh, and he came down too, all of us laughing and punching and kicking and shouting, half on the couch and half on the floor and all the way gone.

"Does this happen often when I'm not around?" We froze. It was Renee, but I couldn't see her. We suspended ourselves in the tangle for a few beats, and then Michel began to giggle. Just a little, but Danny started up too, and soon all three of us were tittering like Japanese schoolgirls. I gasped as we peeled off each other.

Renee stood by the entrance to the kitchen in jeans and a black halter. Her blonde hair was pulled up high on her head, which was cocked to one side at us. She looked great, a perfect ten. But she wasn't black tie.

"Fucked up already, huh?" she said. Danny and I exchanged glances.

"Babe, you're not dressed." Michel stood up and walked over to her with the exaggerated straightness of feigned sobriety.

Our roughhousing had knocked over the bottle of Bacardi, and it was spreading over the hardwood floor. Danny grabbed the sheets of toilet paper from the table and began to swab at the mess. I found my jacket between the cushions of the couch and pulled it out. It was wrinkled pretty badly, but I didn't mind that look. In college I knew a guy whose shirts were perpetually wrinkled, and it always made me feel like he had just come from a better party than the one we were at.

"I can see that," Renee said. "I'm sorry. I didn't know things were so posh tonight." She took Michel's hands in hers. He grabbed them away and leaned against the back of the couch.

"I left you a message about wearing a dress," he said.

"The party is black tie, baby. This isn't a dress."

"I'm sorry, hon," Renee said. "I guess I missed it. I can run home and grab one, if you want. It's not even eight-thirty yet."

"No, you can't do that." Michel's tone was shocked, like Renee had suggested going naked. I went into the kitchen to get paper towel. There didn't seem to be any, so I took two towels from the bathroom. When I came back Renee was yelling.

"How can you be so upset?" she said. "It's nothing! I'll go and get a fucking dress, then meet you down at Atlantis. Why is that such a big deal?" Danny was still on all fours by the spill. I walked over to him and gave him one of the towels. Michel was looking out the window, over the water.

"This is not a big deal," Michel said. He nibbled at his bleeding thumb. His voice was very quiet, like he was talking to himself. "You not getting my message is not a big deal, Renee. The big deal is you always fucking up like this." He paused and ran a hand through his hair. "You're a great girl, and I've known a lot of girls, if you don't mind me saying. You're a big-picture girl, all around you are wonderful, you are fantastic. But you always fuck up these little things, the little details. You can draw the lines, babe, but you can't colour them in, if you get what I'm saying."

"What?" Renee said. "No, I don't get what you're saying. Give me an example, Michel. I mean ..." She choked on a sob, then looked over at Danny and me. I ducked her glance. Danny was guiding his towel in little circles. He was concentrating very hard on the mess.

"You're a loser, Renee," Michel said. "That's what I'm telling you. Life is built on little blocks, little details, and you just can't put it together." He knocked on the window with his knuckles. "You just can't, you're not a builder. And do you know why?"

"Why, Mich? Tell me why, why am I such a loser? Because

I don't walk around with my dick in my hand, is that it?" She was a fighter. That got my respect.

"No," Michel said. Something menacing crept into his whisper. "Because your father fucked you when you were a little girl, and thus you have no mental capacity for things of little import."

We stopped wiping. Danny sighed.

"Fuck you," Renee said. She rocked forward and slapped Michel across the face. The sound reminded me of fat kids' fathers doing belly flops during adult swim.

Danny stood up. Renee holding herself very straight, bracing for Michel's reaction.

"Fuck you, Mich," she said. "You're a fucking dick." I felt embarrassed, like I had opened the bathroom door and caught her pissing.

Michel didn't say anything. Slowly, with all of us watching him, he raised a hand to his face. It was red, but there was no blood. Like I said before, Renee's a little girl. He shook his head at her, turned around and walked away toward the kitchen. Then, like a man who lets the front door close just as he realizes he's forgotten his car keys on the kitchen table, he turned. I could see the line of his jaw from ten feet away. He turned, took two slow steps back toward her, and kicked her in the hip. She crumpled.

Danny and I moved. He came up over the coffee table, I sprinted around the couch. Michel had a second before we made it to him, but he didn't do anything else, just stood over her with his hands against his sides and his shoulders shaking. We tackled him properly this time, each grabbing a shoulder and knocking him down into the kitchen, pinning him against the white linoleum.

"Fuckfuckfuckfuckfuck," Danny said. I agreed with him. My high was gone, at least briefly. Michel looked up at us with blurry eyes.

"What the fuck did you do?" I said to him. He smiled at me. His lips were trembling. "Mich," I said. "Mich. Mich! Fucker." I snapped my fingers over his nose. Our knees were on his shoulders, but he wasn't struggling.

"He's tripping," Danny said. "Look at him, he's gone. Twenty bucks says he was having his own fun before we got here, man. What a crazy ..." His voice trailed off as he looked over his shoulder at Renee. She was curled into a silent ball with her back toward us. It scared me how quiet she was. "We've gotta get her out of here," Danny said. "She just got all kinds of beat up."

"What the fuck did you do?" I said to Michel again.

"I love her," he said. His words were thick and syrupy, as if he was having trouble getting them around his tongue. "Trust me, I love her." The halogen light from the ceiling made the sweat on his face sparkle.

"Right, buddy," Danny said. If there is one thing that makes a drug dealer, it's the ability to take charge when situations get crazy. I was about ready to shit my pants, but Danny was suddenly the definition of all right. He turned to me.

"I'm going to get her home, or to a hospital if she needs it. I don't think he broke anything, but she weighs, like, ninety pounds, so maybe." He stared at her a moment longer, meditating on something, then got up.

Michel didn't try to move. He was taking deep breaths, like he was getting ready to look for something underwater. I mopped at his forehead with my sleeve.

Danny bent down over Renee and put his hand under her chin. He whispered something and she nodded, then tried to stand up. Her leg buckled under the hip Michel had nailed, but Danny bent down and caught her. She screamed. Michel's eyes snapped open.

"Don't let her go," he said to me. "Don't fucking let her go."

"Shut up," I said. He shut up. "Call me when you drop her off," I yelled to Danny.

"Yeah," he shouted back. The door hit the cinder block with a thud. Even from the hall, I could hear Renee sobbing. I looked at Michel. He was still out of it, his eyes shooting all around the kitchen without recognition. I punched him softly in the side of the head.

"What in the fuck is wrong with you?" I said, rising and going to the freezer. It was empty, except for half a bottle of vodka. The fridge wasn't any better. A few energy drinks, a plastic tray of sushi, and some baking soda. I grabbed the vodka. Michel had pulled himself up and was sitting with his back against the pantry.

"I love her, that's all," he said. "I wanted to help her, man." I kneeled against him and pressed the bottle to his cheek. I could feel his heart, a fluttering hummingbird trapped between his ribs. He pulled away, then took the bottle from me and held it there himself.

THE HELMET

WE WERE ON our way back from baseball, Tony not talking because his team had lost, and The Helmet was crossing the street. He was wearing it high on his head, the kind motorbike Nazis wear in movies, and he also had on a Leafs jersey, even though it was the middle of summer and just waking up in the morning was enough to make you sweat. He was talking to himself very fast, so that from our side of the street it looked like he was trying to eat his own lips.

"Leafs suck," Tony yelled at him. But The Helmet kept walking and kept talking, staring at the sidewalk, like he hadn't heard anything. I was ten that summer, but Tony was fourteen and important, and he didn't like it when people didn't listen. "That crazy dick," Tony said under his breath. He rocked on his sneakers like a cobra pulling back to strike, and I took a step away from him in case he decided he needed to hit something.

EVERY SUMMER, our dad sent Tony and me to our mum's place in Dorion, out in the country. Dad worked for the city, driving his truck around Montreal and fixing road signs that had been painted on or knocked over or stolen. His work was harder in the summer, because school was out and kids had more time to cause trouble, and he didn't want us to sit home all day with no one there. So we went to stay with our mum, in the house that was our nana's before our nana died. It had a dog called Alaska, and a yard with two giant trees that worked as goalposts so we could play soccer in the shade.

Dorion wasn't Montreal, though, and we were city boys. Every morning, after checking his face for pimples and his chest for hairs, Tony would go out on the front lawn and pace. It was quiet out there in the country. There were no people on the street corners and no apartments with yelling and not even the all-day hum of cars. In the mornings, when Tony paced the lawn, I could hear him using all the swears we knew, and the thing he swore at was boredom.

"Fuckshitfuck," he said. "This place blows."

"Blows the big one," I called from the patio.

"Exactly," he said. "When we get back to Montreal, Paulie, I'm going to go nuts. I'm going to be unstoppable. I'll drink every beer in the fridge. I'll watch TV until I know the lines to every show. I'll steal the nicest car on the street, and if I drive by a nicer one, I'll switch. I'll go into every club on Ste. Catherine's, especially the naked ones, and when I come out all the girls will be following me."

"Me too," I said.

Our mum made us breakfast and dinner, and we had to be home for those, but she would spend the endless middle of the day in her room with the door closed, making friends on the Internet. So Tony and I had to make the hours pass ourselves. We would go to the beach to look for girls, or to the pier for fishing, or to the depanneur for Mr. Freezies and Humpty Dumpty chips. There was a contest where the letters for H-U-M-P-T-Y D-U-M-P-T-Y were hidden in the bags, but even though I ate at least two a day I could never find a D.

Mostly we would go to the baseball diamond at the edge of town where sometimes there would be a game. I couldn't play, because I was too young, but I was allowed to sit on the bench, and Tony would sit beside me when he wasn't at bat or in the field.

That was the best part of the summer, when Tony would forget that I was only his little brother. In Montreal he had his own friends, bigger boys his own age. They stole Coke and comics from the depanneur, and knew which parts of a girl tasted of candy and which parts tasted of fishsticks. In Montreal he spoke to me only when he needed something done, or when he was mad. Then he would pull down my pants and laugh at my dinger. He said it would never grow unless I got a girl to rub it, and since that would never happen I should learn to tuck it between my legs. He would talk me down until I cried, and if I didn't he would grab my hair and twist it, which was like turning the tap on my eyes.

But in the country, where the bigger boys were the kind who wore overalls and worked on farms and just spoke French, Tony had no problems talking to me. Mostly he would talk about girls, and if he didn't I would ask him to. The girls in the country weren't crazy like the girls in Montreal, he said. City girls would do anything, even sneak away with you to the bathroom at recess so you could go pants off. The country girls were scared, and when Tony took them to the edge of the beach where the rocks were tall and sharp and no one could see, they only ever used their mouths on him, which he said was still good.

When he went to meet the girls, he would take our dad's aftershave, smuggled from the city in his backpack, and rub it all over himself, up his shirt and down his shorts, until his whole body was shining. We never talked about girls when Mum was around, but once she left, Dad started bringing them home, French women with lots of makeup who smelled fancy and drank white wine from a box. After that Tony started thinking about women a lot, so I did too.

But Tony never let me come along to see his girls. I begged and pleaded, because I really needed a girl to rub some size into me before it was too late. But when I tried to follow he would punch me and get upset like we were still in the city. I watched him walk alone to where the road curved into town, my stomach sinking into the space between my socks and my sneakers.

When he left me alone I would practise my hunting. In school we had learned about the San tribe of the Kalahari Desert, and how they are the earth's greatest hunters. Mostly they hunt antelope and the eland, which is like a unicorn with two horns, but really they could hunt anything they felt needed to be killed. The San hunt by pretending they are being hunted too. They guess where their prey will run, and then chase it, sometimes for days, until it is so tired it collapses at their feet. When Tony left me I would hunt like this, chasing Alaska and dodging from tree to tree, closing my eyes, imagining that something was right behind me, hungry for my blood and my insides.

At night, once Tony was home and we were in bed listening to the Expos on the radio, imagining ourselves in the majors, he would tell me the best bits of his adventures, about thongs and necking and spitting and swallowing, especially when I pretended I didn't want to hear.

"Paulie," he would say, "you should've seen me with Emily Poirier today." And if I asked what happened he would say I was too little. But if I said I didn't even know that girl, because I didn't, they all seemed the same to me, he would say, "You do know her, she has tits like fucking watermelons and a real skinny ass." Then I would say, "Doesn't sound so special," and he would tell me how she would drag her tongue all the way from his mouth down below his pants, and while he talked I would rub myself against the bed.

THE LEBEAU TWINS, Stephan and Charles, knew The Helmet's story. For a long time I didn't believe they were twins, because they didn't look the same at all. Charles was a foot taller than Tony even though they were the same age, and his ears stuck out like his head was trying to get rid of them. Stephan was short, the same height as me, and very fat. It was hard to tell where his face ended and his body started. Our mum said they had been born at the exact same time, both of the babies appearing at once, wrestling with each other to get out first. I think Tony was sometimes even a little scared of them — when there was a thunderstorm and every other kid was locked inside, the Lebeau twins were still allowed out to play, and you could hear them over the screams of the wind, whooping and hollering in the rain.

We had heard about The Helmet before. In a small town like Dorion, the crazy people were the famous ones. We knew how he never took it off, and how he talked like a baby, and that he lived in the ghost town out by the church. Our mum had told us how some kids had started making faces at The Helmet from the back of their school bus, and how he had charged the bus with his helmet down, yelling and crying and pounding on its side with his fists all right there in the middle of town.

But the Lebeau twins knew more. Their dad was the bartender at La Garenne, which was built underground with holes in its roof so the cigarette smoke could get out, and was where all the men went on Friday nights. So the twins knew everything. We saw them whenever we went to play.

The English boys would always pick teams against the French ones. Most of us spoke both, but everybody knew who was French and who was English. The French kids were poorer and their dads' cars didn't drive, they just sat on the lawn with their hoods up making the grass die. The English kids had Expos jerseys and aluminum bats and gloves with the signatures of real players inside them. Some of the French kids didn't have gloves at all. Next time we went, while we waited for the game to start, Tony asked the twins to tell us about The Helmet.

"He get that way when he was sixteen." Stephan was chewing a wad of gum, and when he talked you could see it floating in his mouth like a big grey beetle. "He was sixteen and he buy a car right away, a convertible. He drive it along Main, up and down, so everybody they see him. One day he is driving fast, with his head out the window, you know, like a dog. And then he hit some gravel, and the car go to the side, and his head drive, you know, smack! into the mailbox." Charles had been nodding his head along with his brother's story, but at this he jumped up in the air and punched his palm.

"Bam! You believe that?" Charles' ears were red at the edges from the sun. "Just like, whack!" I looked over at Tony, and I could see in his eyes that he was imagining how it would look. Stephan spat his gum out and ground it into the sand. He caught me staring.

"What, you want the gum?" he said. I looked up at Tony, afraid the twins would make me eat it. If Tony hadn't been there, they would have for sure. They hated when a team got short a player and I had to come in and strike out, reaching for the pitches above my head. I imagined the gum, hard and sandy and tasting like plastic, all the things your mouth hates. But Tony reached out with one hand and pushed me back, so I was a little behind him and not important again.

"Keep going about The Helmet," he said. The twins looked at each other, trying to decide which was more fun, the story or bringing me down. But eventually Stephan couldn't hold back.

"People, you know, they were surprised his head was still there at all. He go into surgery for a week, and when he come out, that's it, he is crazy. You know, all the things inside his head they are broken, his brain is finit. And now he wears it, the helmet, so he can keep safe from other mailboxes."

"But how does he get money and stuff?" Tony asked. "How does he eat?"

"Dunno," Stephan said. "Maybe, because he crazy, to eat is not as important."

"Eat his own shit, I bet," Charles said.

Nobody talked for a minute, and then everyone else showed up and we started the game. We lost to the French boys again, even though I never had to play, and again Tony didn't want to talk on the way home.

THAT NIGHT TONY couldn't sleep, and he kept kicking me to make sure I couldn't either. Our blankets were bunched at the end of the bed because it was so hot, and I turned my pillow over and over searching for the cold part.

"I wonder what his head is like, under that helmet," Tony whispered.

"Gross," I said.

"Do you think you can see his brain?"

"He couldn't be alive with his brain out."

"But he is. What about his ears? Does he have ears, or just holes?"

In the next room, we could hear our mum talking on the phone.

"I need to get out of Quebec." She was speaking in both French and English, and it sounded like Montreal. "I feel like I'm at the end of the world here, and if I fell off no one would notice." She laughed, then started coughing. "Europe would be perfect ... I'm in a land of savages here. Barbarians." We heard the zip of the screen door as she took the phone outside to the porch.

"I want to go see him," Tony said.

"If he was in a car crash, how come his face looks fine?"

"That was the surgery. They fixed his face, but they couldn't fix the rest of him. Besides, his face doesn't look fine." He was right, sort of. The Helmet had a big beard, so you couldn't see his cheeks and his chin, and his lips were too red and shiny, like they were made of wax.

"It's a bad idea, Tony," I said.

"Tomorrow," he said. "I want to see what's underneath. We'll go together."

And then he let me sleep.

THE NEXT DAY we drove to the big supermarket out on the highway. Our mum was in a bad mood and was trying not to talk. She didn't tell either of us why, but I figured it had something to do with the marbles. Our dad kept a handful of marbles by the front seat, and whenever he got mad at another car on the road he would pull out in front of them and throw one of the marbles out the sunroof. It made me upset when he did it, because some of the marbles were really good ones — not just cat's eyes but steelies and butterflies and ghosts and shooters.

When I asked Mum why she didn't have any marbles, she asked why I wanted to know, and when Tony told her about Dad she got into that bad mood. Talking about Dad almost always put her in that mood. So once we got to the supermarket I was allowed to run off by myself, because people who are feeling bad always just want to be alone.

Near where I went to find the baseball bats, I found Tony looking at bicycle helmets. There were rows and rows of them, all in different colours, made of foam and plastic and aluminum and mesh. Tony was going over them one by one, pulling them from the shelves and reading their boxes. When he got to the most expensive ones, the kinds for motorbikes that had a visor for your face, he ripped open their boxes and tried them on. He looked like a Lego man, with no neck and a head that was too big for his body.

"Why that one, Paulie?" The mask muffled his voice.

"I dunno," I said. "You picked it."

"No, why does he wear that helmet? His black one. It's a piece of shit, it's older than Nana was." I cringed at this mention of a dead person.

"Maybe that's the only one he has. He can't walk out here to buy a new one, you know."

"But he could get one off a kid," Tony said, and I knew that he'd been thinking about this for a while. "Everyone has bike helmets, and they're all nicer than his. If you were gonna wear something every day, wouldn't you want the best kind?"

"Yeah," I said. I walked down the aisle to the hockey sticks. He kept looking, like the answer was hidden inside one of the boxes.

I KNEW something was wrong when Tony gave me the front seat for the drive home, and as soon as we got on the road he lay down in the back and started to complain about his stomach hurting.

He kept telling Mum that it felt like there were daggers inside it, and when we were almost back home he told her he was going to puke. Tony never got carsick, but as soon as Mum pulled over and opened the door he put his head out over the seat and threw up a little bit on the side of the road. I got out and ran around to look — his barf was purple from the grape juice we'd had in the morning, with tiny bits of Corn Puffs floating around inside its centre. Tony was moaning and clutching his belly. Mum put a hand to his forehead.

"You don't have a fever," she said. Tony just pulled his knees up by his ears and made a sound like he was crying. My mum went to close the door, but he put his hand out and held it open.

"Wait," he said. She looked at her watch.

"Well, throw up again if you're going to do it," she said.

But Tony didn't throw up again, and we just stood there by the side of the road waiting for him. His vomit smelled bad, and I covered my nose with my arm, but I still stared, afraid to turn my back on it. The cars that went by slowed to look at us, but Mum would glare at them and they would keep driving.

"Do it now if you're going to," she said. "I just cleaned the damn car last week."

"Wait," he said.

"Tony, we need to go." She looked at her watch again.

"Let me walk," he said. "I'll walk back with Paulie." She looked at me, then down the road.

"We're a half hour's walk from the house," she said. "You can't do that if you're sick." I looked around. We were at the edge of the graveyard, by the church, and somewhere in my mind I realized what Tony was doing and got nervous. My heart woke up and started to pound very fast.

"I just need some fresh air," he said. "I'm carsick."

I collected all the bravery I had into one piece and did my best to help him.

"We can walk from here," I said. "Tony knows the way." Mum looked at me. Her face was drawn tight, and I could see all the lines on it. She looked old, and I couldn't imagine how she had once been a girl like the ones Tony and I wanted. I couldn't imagine her as anything but a mum, someone who carried you in from the car when you fell asleep on a ride home at night.

"Dad would let us." When Tony said that, Mum's face got even tighter, like she needed to go to the bathroom, and then she let out a long breath.

"Okay," she said, fast and very quietly. "If that's what you two want."

Tony climbed out of the car, stepping over the drying vomit, and she got back in and drove away. We watched the car leave, not saying anything. When they vanished around the corner, Tony reached into his pocket and pulled out one of her cigarettes and some matches.

"How did you make yourself throw up?" I said.

"Finger in my throat," he said. "It's easy." His hair was matted down with sweat, and he looked very cool, his jeans riding low and his black T-shirt loose and wrinkled.

"Oh. Which way do we go?" I said. He pointed and we walked, through the graveyard. Most kids would have been scared, but the graves were all just crosses and tombstones, not like the graveyard in Montreal, up on the hill, which had angels and stone swords and big buildings with no doors. That graveyard made me nervous — I closed my eyes when we drove by it — but this one just seemed sad, like no one cared about the dead people there anymore. Tony's cigarette was broken near the base, and he had to hold a finger over the crack to use it. He leaned his head back and blew the smoke straight up, like women do in the movies. When we reached the edge of the graveyard, he went to rub it out on a tombstone, but then stopped and took one more drag before throwing it away into the grass. We were only a few hundred feet from the woods, and I put my hands into my pockets so Tony wouldn't see them shaking.

As we got closer I could see the buildings of the ghost town. A long time ago, before our mum and dad were alive and when there was a World War, someone built a city where the soldiers could practise their fighting. The twins had told us about it. But this was the first time we had seen the ghost town up close. There were only three buildings, all grey and made of cement. When the war ended nobody took them away, so they had stood there forever, and now weeds grew up their walls and through the holes they had for windows and into the marks in their sides that explosions must have made. Two of them had no roofs, and a tree grew up the middle of one, making it look like the house where the Keebler Elves lived.

Tony went straight to the one that was covered, as if he already knew what was inside. It was dark past the little door, and when he went in he disappeared and I cried after him: "Tony!"

"Shut up!" he yelled back, and I followed him. There was just one room, with a very high ceiling, and inside it, by the light coming through the holes in the wall, we saw where The Helmet must have lived. It stank like a toilet that someone had left a shit in overnight. Chip wrappers were everywhere, all turned out so their shiny silver insides were showing. The earth was sunken in the centre of the room, and there was a pile of blankets where it got lowest.

"A foxhole ..." Tony whispered. Then he saw it, in the far corner of the room, upside down and discarded. The helmet. He went and grabbed it, holding it up toward the sunshine streaming in. I ran over to stand beside him, to get my own look and run my hand over it. Inside was some padding, worn down to tiny brown squares, and the outside was hard, made of something that felt like metal covered in hundreds of tiny bumps. Tony put it on his head and turned to show me how it looked, but his mouth fell open and I knew right away what was behind me.

The Helmet filled in the door. I could tell it was him by his beard. His head was bald, like Tony had predicted, and shiny, but I couldn't see any scars on it, or on either side of what looked like very normal ears. But I did see for the first time how his eyes were funny, how one was set higher up than the other and how they didn't both look in the same direction. He was wearing jeans rolled up to the knees and no shirt, and his chest was hairy and you could see all his ribs. He looked at us with the one eye that worked, and then slowly he spoke.

"*Mien*." His mouth went crazy after he said it, opening and closing and moving around like he was trying to get a taste out. I stood still, because I was too afraid to move. "*C'est le mien*," he said again.

The Helmet was taller than me and Tony together, and all I could think of was him charging forward and beating us like we were a school bus. But Tony didn't seem scared. He walked toward The Helmet, carefully putting one foot before the other, until he was right in front of him. And then he held the helmet out.

As The Helmet reached down for his prize, Tony swung. He brought it up, straight into The Helmet's nose, who let out a yelp that sounded like Alaska when Tony kicked her, and fell back into the wall. Tony threw the helmet down and ran out. I went to follow him, but the sight of The Helmet lying there froze me at the door. Blood was pumping from his nose down into his mouth, turning his teeth red.

The blood I was used to was bright and thin, the kind that came away on my hand when I skinned a knee or bit off too much of one of my nails. This blood was different, dark and syrupy. I had only seen it once before, when my friend Mario had fallen off the slide at school and cracked his head on the pavement. He had lain still while it leaked slowly out his ear, and we had all stood and watched, not knowing what to do, until our teacher Mrs. Phaneuf ran over and made us all wait inside while an ambulance came and took Mario away.

The Helmet reached out and grabbed my arm, and I screamed. He was very strong, even sitting down, and when I went to pull away my feet played a trick on me and I fell into the dirt. The Helmet used his other hand to grab my leg and pull me toward him. I screamed again, and then Tony was there, kicking The Helmet's arm away.

"Get up!" he yelled at me, and his hands were under my shoulders, lifting me up the way I thought only our dad could do. Then we were running, side by side, even though his legs were much longer, and we weren't looking back. I tried to close my eyes, to be like the San in the desert. But as we ran away from the buildings, toward the graveyard, I realized it would be impossible to run all the way home. Sooner or later, we would have to slow down.

A BAD LAKE FOR FISHING

THE BRUISES ARE coming in, violent and purple and ugly. They are ten hours old, preening like girls on September's first day of school. But I ignore them. I grab the skirt off the floor and pull it to my waist. It's real silk, and it feels like a feather against the inside of my thigh. This is how I look when my father opens the door: almost naked, covered in bruises, holding a skirt over my crotch.

———

THEY HAD BEEN waiting for me in the bathroom during lunch. Usually I went in right after fourth period, before eating, to wash my hands. But that day I went to my locker first and then down to the band room to collect some music, so they must have been waiting a while. Their impatience probably made it worse.

I had my head down, or I would have seen them in the mirror. But I was checking for dirt under my fingernails when a beefy red arm clamped over my mouth. It smelled pungent, like curry powder. Adam Maslowski. Taller than most of our teachers and still dressed warmly in his baby fat, his red hair complemented by freckles the size of dimes.

He didn't bother covering my eyes. Identifying my tormentors was useless. I'd tried, the first time, but the administration seemed to consider beatings to be just part of the high school experience. Adam was suspended for a day. That had only made them beat harder the next time; since then I've been both a rat and a queer.

"Fucking faggot, coming in here to beat off before lunch." If Maslowski hadn't been such a great unified mass already, Hollis James could have been his other half. Hollis was Asian, and even taller than Adam, but skinny. Sleepy eyes and a thin mouth gave his face a kind of reptilian look, highlighted by the incredible tightness of his skin. As if his soul were pulling on his face from behind his eyes. You could fit golf balls in the hollows of his cheeks.

"He is a fucking faggot," Adam said. "He's coming in here to think about dick. Aren't you, faggot?" He dragged me down to the floor of the bathroom, keeping his forearm between my teeth. I felt the tickle of his hair against the roof of my mouth.

"Dirty faggot, dicks are for kids." Hollis pulled back a bunched fist and slammed me in the stomach. I doubled over, but Adam held me flat against the tiles. Hollis hit me again, in the chest, and then in the kidneys. My throat filled with bile.

"What the fuck? He's throwing up on me!" Adam tore his arm away. I yelled and vomited at the same time. There were thin trails of blood among the mess. Adam grabbed my hair and pulled my head back, then reached into his pocket and pulled out a rag. Balling it up, he shoved it in my mouth. Gasoline and sour milk. Someone stepped into the bathroom behind him, saw what was going on, and left. Hollis grabbed my arms and held them behind my back. Adam just looked at me, his eyes wild. They paused for a few moments like that, catching their breath. I don't think they knew what to do next.

"He's a cocksucker, Adam," Hollis whispered through clenched teeth. It was a reminder.

"That's right, he is, isn't he? Well …" Adam undid his fly and pulled his hooded penis over the elastic of his boxers. He shook it in my face. I kept my head down. He waddled closer, holding it out to within a few inches of my nose.

"Want to suck it?" he said. He pissed without waiting for an answer.

"What the fuck?" Hollis cried. "Shit, yes!" He laughed while Adam sprayed my nose, my lips, my eyes, my hair. I squinted as tightly as I could, but I still felt the burning. They were laughing all around me. I heard Adam zip up, then Hollis slammed me between my shoulder blades. I fell face first back onto the tiles and he stepped over me, toward the door. Adam was already halfway into the hall.

"Queer cunt."

—

THEY WERE SURER about that than I was. There had only been one guy up to that point, and everything about it had been so hesitant, so subtle. Like getting taller, it was a change that happened so slowly I never noticed it taking place.

I had worked at a Safeway the summer before, stocking shelves and mopping aisles. Labouring at night, alone under the neons, the job was torture by inanity. But my mother wanted me to do it, so I spent three months there.

Derek was a cashier, just barely in his twenties. I had admired him since my first day, when he had taken me around and shown me the basics of the work. His hair was gelled up in a kind of faux-hawk; he was always very put together. He had his lip pierced, and would wear a leather jacket over his uniform when the store manager wasn't on duty. We took breaks together, smoking cigarettes by the loading bay, and I asked him the kind of questions you normally pose to a brother, or maybe your sister's boyfriend. Just crap about high school and being a teenager. I asked him only once about girls. The store was closed, and we were sitting in the frozen foods section to escape the humidity of the night's heat.

"Girls, girls, girls," he said. He had a habit of repeating words as he mulled a question. He spoke very slowly, too, measuring out his sentences syllable by syllable. For whatever reason, I attributed a great deal of wisdom to him because of this. "To be honest, pal, I've never had much luck with girls."

"Really?" I said, my mouth hanging open dumbly. He had long hair, it was always falling down over his eyes, a look I thought every girl desired.

"The truth. I don't know if maybe it's my game, but I've never been too good with girls. Girls and classes, those were my Kryptonite in high school."

"Me too," I said, even though I had excellent grades.

"My type of guy," he laughed, pushing his hair up out of his eyes.

He was an excellent listener, even when I would ramble — always pushing for more, questioning me as we unpacked Campbell's soup and refilled the flour bins. It thrilled me how my opinions would affect him, make him purse his lips and think.

Eventually our breaks moved to his car, an old maroon Nissan Sentra, where we would listen to Nirvana and Everlast and smoke the roaches he kept in a bag in his glove box. I took short drags and rarely inhaled, but Derek would roll his window down and blow rings out toward the red glow of the Safeway sign.

One night, near the end of the summer, he reached over and put his hand on my knee. I didn't move it, and when he looked at me after a few moments I gave him a kind of half nod. The steering wheel of the car seemed enormous, almost as if it was growing in front of him. We kissed a bit, and did some touching that amounted to something like a handjob. We only had fifteen minutes for break, though, and when I came back the next evening to work my final shift, Derek wasn't scheduled.

—

I DON'T KNOW HOW, but when school started up again, they knew. I wasn't dressing or acting differently, I didn't stick a rainbow triangle to my locker, but they knew. Maybe I spaced out in class one day, and when the teacher asked what I did during the summer I unknowingly replied, "Oh, well, I went to Edmonton for a week, bought a PlayStation, and had my first homosexual experience. In the front seat of a Nissan."

—

MY MOTHER, perhaps, has some idea. She grew up in New York, with a pretty liberal family, and she has some gay friends from when she used to volunteer at the local playhouse. I think she might even be pleased if I told her; she might think it made me special in some way.

One Sunday night we were watching *60 Minutes*, and a story came on about a high school quarterback in Texas who had come out to his teammates.

"What a brave boy," she said as the show cut to a commercial. "I can't imagine how strong he must be to do something like that." Then she turned and looked at me, suddenly anxious for my reply.

"Yeah," I said. It was dark outside, and we're one of those families that turns off the lights when they watch television, so she couldn't see me getting red. "I bet his friends aren't so supportive when the camera's not around."

"What do you mean?" she said, although she must have known.

"I mean nobody wants to look like a hick on national television, Mom. But I'll bet they all run out of the shower when he takes his towel off." She laughed.

"Oh," she said, "you're being silly. People are very understanding these days, you know." But I couldn't tell if she believed it. Then my father came in and we switched to the game, because he hates Ed Bradley.

My father always seems uncomfortable around me, as if I was a misaddressed package that just arrived at his house one morning. He says "son" with everything — How was your day, son? Did you take care of your mother, son? You need to spend more time in the fresh air, son — like he is trying to familiarize himself with the word.

We fish together. But even then we're only content, never happy. He is satisfied that he's being a good father, bringing his son out on the lake to build our relationship in silence. I feel pleased that I'm being a dutiful son, sacrificing a day to placate my father. But neither of us ever catches anything, and no real bonding ever goes on. Maybe it's a bad lake for fishing.

—

NOW MY FATHER stands in the doorway, framed by the light from the hall. He doesn't move. He doesn't say anything. The overhead light is off; I only have my reading lamp on, and it occurs to me that maybe he can't see me.

"Justin?" His voice doesn't sound right. It's strained, but more than that ... it's like someone has their hands around his throat and he's struggling to force the words out. He steps forward, then falters and places his hand on the wall. I keep quiet, drop my mother's clothes on the floor, and sit back on the bed. He turns on the light and comes in. His face suddenly looks older.

"Justin," he says. I wonder if he thinks he's dreaming. Slowly, he turns around, studying each part of the room like it's a museum exhibit. The posters of various sports stars on one wall. My fishing rod, in the corner by my hockey stick. My bookshelf, packed with Dragonlance and Forgotten Realms novels. He looks everywhere but at the foot of the bed, where the clothes lie in a wrinkled pile. I cross my legs and sit on my duvet, suddenly very aware of my own nakedness.

"Your chest is bruised," he says.

I nod. I feel scared, for both of us.

He moves closer to the bed and steps on the bra. Its underwire snaps beneath his weight. He pulls back and looks down, then bends over. He picks up the skirt. His eyes look confused behind his thick glasses.

"Your mother wore this the first time I met her parents," he said. "I'll bet you didn't know that."

"No, Pa, I didn't." My hands are shaking violently. My mouth tastes metallic.

"This skirt and a purple blouse," he says. "Your grandfather wasn't too impressed by me. But your mother ... she was so pretty back then, son. Still is."

I look at the floor, at the door behind him, anywhere but where he is.

"These are her clothes," he says. "They shouldn't be here,

in your room." His manner is still distant, and his words come out slow and heavy. If I didn't know better, I'd think he was stoned. "I'll take them with me," he says, and pads slowly to the door. He stops there, and turns to look back at me. "These are her clothes," he says again, and then closes the door softly behind him.

HOME MOVIES

JULIUS SAUVAGE was born in Montreal, a beautiful son to two ordinary parents. His father worked in the garment district, stitching ready-to-wear dresses for Westmount beauty queens. His mother sold newspapers on the street corner outside their apartment. Julius shared a bed with his parents until the day he moved away, his eighteenth birthday. After that, he never saw them again, but they thought about him every day.

Julius went west, over the mountains and into the sunshine. The year was 1960. He rode railcars all the way, and watched Canada slip by in a blur of frontiers and the men chasing them. When he hit the ocean he turned south, toward the sun and golden promise of California.

Julius acted in Los Angeles, mostly because he could. His face was all smooth ebony angles, and there will always be work for the beautiful wanderers. He played a cowboy, the first black hero of the silver screen. He would sign autographs with a J so exaggerated you could cut yourself on its curve. He thought himself in Eden.

Julius married a petite woman named Frances, mesmerized by the many faces of her eccentricity. She wrote only with crayons. He fell in love with her the way you fall in love with a child, all at once and for no reason. She killed herself a year later, jumping in a sundress the colour of ketchup from a balcony at the Chateau Marmont.

Julius himself died thirty years later, when old age arrived to reinforce his broken heart. He went quietly, on a rainy Sunday morning, curled up in a blue velvet armchair by a window facing the street. He had faded, like the ink on a Golden Age comic, his adventures forgotten and gathering dust.

Julius and Frances had one son, Harold. Julius gave him all the finest things, and read him bedtime tales about Greek gods and true love. Sometimes, when the boy would creep into his father's room late at night, he would catch Julius crying. For the rest of his life, he would carry this as evidence of how wonderful a woman his mother had been.

When he was eighteen Harold left Julius to go to school, then dropped out and became a carpenter. Julius stopped talking to him after that, telling Harold carpenters could only ever lead lives that left them wishing. Harold knew his father was wrong, because Jesus never wanted, and who could ask for more than that?

Harold married Bernadette in the fall of that year. He kept a leaf from that day in his wallet, and even when it dried it did not crumble or break. Bernadette still had all her baby teeth, and made everyone she met feel like they could stay up all night with her, just talking with the lights off and holding hands beneath the blankets.

Harold took to collecting stamps, pasting them slowly into the pages of his favourite book, making sure they lined up as squarely as fascists on parade. Bernadette warned him that soon he wouldn't be able to read the book anymore, but Harold said he loved it so much he wanted to send the whole world the words.

Harold and Bernadette had a girl, Marianne, probably a few years sooner than they should have. Her eyes were so bright Harold would sometimes turn off all the lights in the room to make sure they didn't glow. *My Marianne*, he would tell people, *she's a miracle*. He kept her away from heights, and away from heartache, and sang her to sleep until she grew too old.

HERE BE MONSTERS

I'M TRYING TO switch radio stations and drive and smoke all at the same time, and the reality that this is impossible finally dawns when I drop a lit cigarette into my lap. I should grab it before it burns the seat or my crotch, but instead I keep one hand on the wheel and the other on the radio dial, because I'm desperate to find just one decent song. This truck doesn't have a CD player, or even a tape deck, and that's really bothering me, because I feel like for some reason it would make a big difference if I could spend tonight listening to something I've heard before.

Finally I find a station playing the Chili Peppers, and even though they don't have anything new out, I decide that's good enough and grab the cigarette from between my legs and look up and Danny's car is still right there, two in front of mine, slowing down for a yellow light. I've been surprised by how cautiously he drives ever since he left his apartment — never straying into the left lane on the highway, indicating every time he makes a turn, keeping a very consistent fifteen feet between the car in front of him and his own, a black Infiniti G35 with tan interior and

19-inch rims. The rims never stop spinning, even when the wheels they rest on are idle.

At the next light Danny makes a left, but the two cars between us aren't turning, so I have to hustle a bit to catch up with him. Some punks jump into the street, teenagers on their way to sit outside a Tim Hortons for the night. They're all in black, of course, so I nearly hit one, and when I slam on the brakes and then slowly pull around him the kid pounds on the trunk with his fist. On any other night I'd pull over, just to send him running, but I don't want to lose track of Danny. We've never met, but Danny is very important to me.

Finally, after several more turns, he slows down and parks in a row of sedans by the side of the road. The door of the Infiniti opens as I pull by, but I avoid looking at him and decide to go around the block once. I have time. He'll come back to his car when he's finished whatever he's doing inside. And I'll be waiting for him.

When I was eleven, I hit a walk-off home run to give the Surrey Storm a comeback victory in the Vancouver Little League Championships. The bat I used, a wooden Louisville Slugger, a present from my grandfather, is sitting, wrapped in blankets, between the two front seats of my car. Tonight I will use it to shatter every bone in Danny Marconi's body. I will beat him until his flesh turns to paste, until every bone in his body cracks like a double toward centre field, until I am so covered in his blood that it mixes with my own. I will beat him until I no longer have the strength to raise the bat above my head, and then it will be over.

IT WAS THE beginning of September, the days were just gaining that pleasant end of summer urgency. The evenings cooled to the point where you felt perfectly comfortable in a sweater and shorts. Mya Carter had just finished her first week of the tenth grade.

She was a beautiful girl, with eyelashes so long she had to trim them lest she tickle her cheeks when she closed her eyes to sleep. Maybe to celebrate the end of their first week in school, Mya and two friends, Avery and Jodie, took some pills and went to a party on Tsawwassen Beach, where you can walk back and forth over the American border. Dozens of kids gathered around fires in garbage cans, reggaeton blaring from a stereo stuffed with D batteries. Although this is not an important detail, on that night Mya was wearing a blue hooded sweatshirt and a white skirt.

At some point, likely near midnight, Mya collapsed. Avery and Jodie were dancing beside her and it seemed like she had tripped, but when they reached down to help her up they saw how her eyes had rolled back into her head, how the whites were bulging in their sockets. They pulled her away from the crowd, away from the beach, back toward the bluff and the road where so many sedans were parked. As they laid her down, she vomited a hot mix of blood and bile down her chin and across the front of her hoodie. Screaming, the girls dialed 911, summoning an ambulance and scattering the party into countless basements and garages. Three hours later, in a very quiet hospital, the drugs finished Mya off. Her face, when I saw it, had gone pale and slack, like a wax bust left out in the sun.

A week earlier, Jodie had been out to dinner with her parents at one of Tsawwassen's fancier restaurants, a small Italian place run by a retired New York auctioneer. Midway through dinner Jodie went to the bathroom, and stepped out the back door to check the messages on her cell phone. There she met a waiter who sold her nine hits of Ecstasy. That waiter, the son of the retired auctioneer, was Danny Marconi. For that reason, tonight, he and I are destined to meet.

I PARK SEVERAL hundred feet away from Danny and wait. Aside from his, the cars are all mid-nineties sedans, which is how you can tell the age of the people inside the party. Adult gatherings have minivans and SUVs. Another car pulls up every few minutes and kids stream out like insects from beneath a log, five from each back seat. I start to get a little cold but don't want to turn the motor on, so I pull my arms inside my shirt and try to slow down my breathing. A spider slowly makes its way across my windshield, and, like everything, it makes me think of her.

A cop drives by, very slowly. He's looking toward the house, so he doesn't notice me slumped in the cab of the truck. Another patrol car follows maybe ten seconds later, with different plates. They're checking the place out too, getting ready to pay the party a visit of their own. It's a Tuesday night; no one else in this town can be causing trouble. An imaginary noise complaint is all they need to walk up to the front door, and then the party will write its own ticket. I swear beneath my breath — Danny's dealing inside, and I can't let the cops find him. Two years trading cigarettes is far better than he deserves. I need to get to him first. He is mine, and I'll piss on him to prove it. I get out of the truck and reach back for the bat, then reconsider and leave it inside.

I move through the bushes, come out into the backyard of the house. It's a bigger place, California modern, and all the lights are on. On the patio a few kids are passing a joint and drinking beers, talking about hockey. They look underage, and barely glance over as I move into the porch light.

"Cops," I say, and they understand right away, some heading toward the trees, others going inside. One says, "Thanks," as he passes me, but doesn't look me in the eyes. I let myself in the back door behind them. Four more guys are playing poker at the kitchen table, one with a girl on his lap. She's blonde, in a little pink halter top that shows her shoulders, covered in freckles. The guys are older, mid-twenties, all wearing yellow Livestrong bracelets. The only one worth mentioning is a musclehead wearing a tight white T-shirt and board shorts. He has a tattoo of a polar bear on his forearm. There's a television on the kitchen counter behind them. A European poker tournament is playing with the sound off.

"Cops," I say. They shrug. They look ugly and pathetic, strategizing over twenty dollars on a Saturday night. An empty case of Molson Export is lying on its side at their feet. The girl is watching me, and I feel like maybe, somehow, she knows.

"What's going on?" she says. The guy whose lap she's on looks over his shoulder, scans me up and down, then turns back to the game.

"Cops are coming," I say. "Almost here." She nods dumbly, her mouth hanging open. Fourteen, if I had to guess. I turn my back on her, move down a hallway. I come across a room entirely bare, except for a desk lamp with no lampshade, plugged in and turned on, and a cardboard standup of Boba Fett. I wonder who owns this house. I can hear music throbbing from somewhere below me. The real party must be in the basement. I'm starting to sweat, worrying that I might not find Danny in time, and I feel my hair growing damp at the roots.

Then a locked door. I knock, but there's no answer, even though I can see light coming from beneath it. I knock again, and when nothing happens I throw my weight into it. It gives with a crack, and I fall into an empty bathroom. There's a mirror on the counter by the sink, but nothing else. The wallpaper in the bathroom is garish, millions of tiny pink and purple umbrellas, and it makes me dizzy.

"Hey, hey, what are you doing, man?" The voice is behind the shower curtain, which pulls back to reveal Danny, his pants down.

He is tiny, far smaller than I imagined, and his pale, skinny legs stick out from beneath his dress shirt, which is just long enough to conceal his cock. He, too, is wearing one of the yellow rubber bracelets. His leather jacket is draped over the toilet. A girl is on the floor of the tub, hastily pulling on her jeans, her red hair falling over her face.

"Danny." I don't mean to say it, not like that, but he's surprised me.

"Yeah, yeah, hey," he says. He points down at the girl. "A little busy, man. Give me ten minutes, alright? Then I'll take care of you. Promise."

"Cops," I say. My knees are shaking, I've lost my cool. "The cops are here, we've gotta go."

"Fuck," he says. "Right, let's do it. Give me one minute." He doesn't seem to wonder how I know his name, such is his little man's arrogance. That's fine.

"Sure," I say. I step outside and try to close the door again, but it's broken now and won't stay closed. I let the door go. In the hallway there is a framed map of a coastline. The map is very old, an antique, and has dragons and giant squid pencilled inside patches of the water, with the words *Here Be Monsters* beside them. Something about these pictures calms me, and I close my eyes and take some deep breaths, sucking in air, filling myself with the smell of stale beer that permeates the house. Think of Mya, the curve of her chin, the way she talked when she was sleepy. I miss her.

The map's glass holds my reflection, and I'm repulsed by the dark hollows beneath my eyes. I didn't sleep at all last night, the third night in a row. Whenever I closed my eyes, my thoughts became animated, like I was trying to dream in cartoon. The colours were so lurid I started to feel sick. I wondered what

Danny was doing, decided that he was probably in some club downtown with an Asian girl and a Prada suit, escaping to the washroom every half hour for a caterpillar-sized line and a chance for a good cry. I hoped he was crying.

I tried to find something on television, but every channel was just static, black-and-white and endless, and after several minutes I realized that the cable must be out. I grabbed a pack of cigarettes and went outside onto the front porch and then the lawn. I had two smokes and went back inside and *Little Caesar* had come on the television. As I finally fell asleep I kept seeing Eddie Robinson crying, "Is this the end of Rico?" over and over and over again.

The bathroom door opens and Danny comes out, wiping his nose.

"Where're the cops?" he says. He has very full, womanly lips. Almost in answer, red and blue flashes appear on the wall at the end of the hall, which must face the front of the house. "Shit, I'm parked right at the end of the driveway, man." This is true, I saw him park there.

"We can wait in my car," I say. "It's farther up the road."

"Yeah, good, I like that," Danny says. We go back the way I came, through the kitchen. The girl in the pink top is still there, face down on a couch in the breakfast nook. The poker slobs are gone, and the channel on the television has been changed to a cooking show. Out the back doors, onto the patio, and into the woods.

"Thanks for the help in there, man," Danny says. "Kind of a bummer, though. That girl was a hot one. I love redheads, they're the best. All the stories are true."

"Yeah," I say. I'm getting giddy, glad that Danny can't see me smiling in the dark.

"What's your name, man?"

"Rupert," I tell him, although it isn't.

"Great name, man. Real old school, I like that. Like the bear."

"What?"

"The white bear. Rupert the bear, man. You never heard of that? This little bear, he could talk, and he had adventures and shit."

"No," I tell him, "I've never heard of that." This is true.

We reach the edge of the woods and I throw a hand up while I look beyond the ditch onto the road. The cops are maybe a hundred and fifty feet away, two cars, lights on. No one else, though — they must be inside, or hanging out at the door. I point my truck out to Danny, and we walk slowly across the road, doing nothing to attract attention. He hops in the cab.

"That's me," he says, pointing to the Infiniti. One of the patrol cars is parked directly in front of it, and as Danny points a cop wanders back from the house and grabs a radio. He barks into it, standing silhouetted in the middle of the street.

I AM BREATHING very fast. Danny is in my car, and right now it would be so easy. The bat is inches from his hand, lying between us, but he takes no notice of it. He rubs his nose and sniffs twice, rampant from the drugs.

"Cops, man, I fucking hate them," he says. "Good thing there aren't too many of them here. Fuck, two cars, that must be every cop in Tsawwassen."

I don't say anything.

"Not like New York," he continues. The less I talk the more he seems to need to fill the space. "Cops everywhere in New York. Safest city in the world now, man. You know those pictures, with the taxis, all taxis? It's like that now with cops there, all cops." He pauses for a second, and I can feel him looking at me in

the half light of the cab. "You ever been to New York?" he says. His voice is a staccato whisper, firing out of him without direction or control.

"No," I tell him. I slide my hand around the shaft of the bat. "Tell me about it."

"It's the best, man, you've gotta go. Best place in the world, centre of the fucking universe. You wouldn't believe it. Civilization, it's beautiful, everywhere. They ran out of room going side to side, so they started going up, toward the sky, you know? There's energy in the streets, they stink of it. Pure energy, human lifeforce. It's amazing, stops your heart." He is staring straight ahead now, imagining New York through my windshield.

"I'll go," I say. "One day." My head is pounding with blood, it is urging me on, and part of me wants to start the car so I can put some music on for this.

"You have to. Gotta do it. Must. There's a hotel there, the St. Regis, you heard of that? The St. Regis Hotel?" He cracks his knuckles. My shirt is stuck to my back with sweat.

"No, don't," I tell him. I try to lift the Slugger slowly, but it's caught on something in the back seat, one of the blankets.

"Yeah, well, it's some spot. Where all the celebrities go. Not all the celebrities, actually, just the classy ones. On 55th and Fifth, baby. Tucked away, you'd never see it if you weren't looking for it, but it's there. I stayed two nights, when I went to New York. Cost me like fifteen hundred bucks, but it was worth it. Everything there is perfect, made for guys like us, for fucking gentlemen. Sheets so soft they make a baby seem hard. Paintings everywhere, really old ones, classics." He sighed. "The St. Regis, man."

"Sounds great," I say. "Real nice, I'm sure." *Guys like us.* He is pouring his heart out to me and I have no choice but to let him finish, because there isn't enough room in the cab to get a good swing in, and I don't want blood on my seats. I'll have to wait until the cops leave.

"One day I'm going to own that hotel," he's saying. "Call me old fashioned, call me a romantic, but one day ..." He slouches down in the seat and licks his lips, in awe of his vision. "I'll take a room on the top floor and hold the best party in town, every Saturday night — and the best party in New York is the best party in the world. I'll have butlers bringing the drugs around on platinum trays, and girls everywhere, so thick you can't move without stepping on them. And everybody who's in there, everybody, they'll have to wear white. Only white. Everyone in New York'll know my name then. Danny Marconi, King of the St. Regis." I laugh, I'm shocked by how childlike he is. I wonder what other secrets he has, what things are kept inside a man like him.

"I can see it," I tell him.

"Really?" he says. "Thanks." His eyes are bloodshot and squinting, but there is hope in them, and part of me begins to feel a little sad.

Later, looking back, I realized this should have been when I reconsidered things. A decent person, one with some sense of mercy, would have let their blood lust subside here, would have paused for a moment to consider whether they deserved to pass judgment on another man's life. But it never even crossed my mind.

Two more cops appear at the end of the driveway. Between them is the hulk from the poker table, roaring like a chained animal. I think of the polar bear on his forearm.

"This won't be pretty, my friend," Danny says. The cops are struggling to push him into the back of their car. Some of his friends come running out behind them, but they aren't drunk enough to intercede, so they just stand back and yell at the cops, one of them doing the you-must-be-kidding-me laugh that kids do when cops are around, and I think, if I were a cop, I'd find that laugh pretty insulting. The two cops wrestling with the guy aren't tiny, but they aren't close to as big as he is and even though they're kicking at his legs and pushing him down by his neck, they can't force him somewhere he doesn't want to go. Then his head hits the doorframe, and there's this very familiar sound, the pop of something hitting a car, a tennis ball even, and he's knocked out, falling over, and they slide him in and close the door.

"Gonna feel that in the morning, huh?" Danny says.

I don't say anything. It looks like the cops are satisfied with their work, and they get into the cars and flick the lights off, preparing to drive away. The kids give them a last round of heckling and then turn back to the house. My heart starts beating faster; I can feel it coming on now. Even as the first cop car rounds the corner at the end of the road, Danny is already opening the door of the truck.

"Thanks a lot, man," he says. "I appreciate the bail out. Danny Marconi owes you one, anytime. It's a promise." I grab the bat as he's closing the door, then jump out my own side, keeping it tight against my leg, then come around the front of the car. He's still stoned, buzzing like he's been set to vibrate, so when he leaps out of the cab he botches his landing slightly. He rights himself, looks up, and I am there.

The first swing is one-handed, from my hip, but I catch him on the chin and he flies backwards. Then I am over him, two-handed, just as I've imagined it. Crunching his head, again and again. I close my eyes. The first blow has shattered his jaw, and all he can make is a faint mewling sound, one that quickly fades into a symphony of cracks and duller, wetter sounds. It is beautiful, erotic, and I can feel my clothes becoming damp with his blood. It spatters onto my face, into my hair, and it feels like a cold shower after a day at the beach, filled with the promise of renewal. I am crying, too, sobbing, and this only makes me swing harder, over and over, until the bat is making contact with the road, sending shockwaves of pain through my arms as the wood hits the pavement. I open my eyes and see, through the tears, victory.

My senses and surroundings come back slowly, and I look around, back at the driveway down the road, over the other cars parked only feet away from me. But there is no one here. I throw the bat, stained black in the dark, into the bed of the truck, and then I flee. I do a three-point turn over his body, feeling what must be his ribs burst beneath the weight of the wheels.

My hands on the wheel are soaked, red fills all their tiny crevices. I roll the window down, turn the radio on. The air that flows in is cold, it dries the sweat on my face. Again I think of Mya, and for the first time she makes me smile. I remember a few summers ago, when we were both up at the cabin in Kelowna. One morning, after she'd been swimming, she dragged me down to the laundry room. There was a bucket in the corner, and she pointed at it. She kept going, "Look! Look!" but wouldn't even move past the doorway herself. Inside the bucket was a massive spider, a beast the size of my fist, and when I leaned over I could see strands of something wet dangling between its jaws. There was bleach on top of the washing machine, but when I grabbed it and went to pour some over the thing Mya began to scream. She said she never would have showed me if she had known what I would do, and I apologized and we went back upstairs, leaving it alone in its lair. But later, when she was outside on the lake, I went back down with a handful of paper towel and crushed the beast, surprised at the sound it made when I folded the sheets around its swollen belly. That night, when she went to look at it again and couldn't find it, I told her it must have escaped, found a way back out into the night. She laughed, and the promise of its freedom thrilled her.

A KIND OF DIGNITY

"REMEMBER," Deo said, "Proust said we are healed from suffering only when we experience it in full. Don't hide your grief, my friend." We embraced again as he and his brother Ares left my father's funeral. His cheek was moist against my own. They moved awkwardly toward the temple door, taking exaggerated steps around clusters of old Jewish men.

MY FATHER'S CANCER had pounded him like water against a rock — its pace was lethargic, but there was no question that it would eventually break through.

The funeral was a relaxed affair. Ties were loosened, my uncle and mother made speeches, and the laughs outnumbered the tears.

When the ceremony had concluded, Deo and Ares approached me. My father had worked at their restaurant, Athena, when he had first come to Canada, waiting tables while he was in graduate school. When he left he moved from valued employee to favourite customer. Athena was where my birthday dinners were held when I was growing up.

"Joshua," Deo said. His eyes were red and wet. I embraced them both.

"I'm happy you two could make it."

"Of course," Ares said. He dragged his hand across his mouth. "He was very close to both of us, your father."

"A beautiful man," Deo said. "He was one of the most beautiful people I've ever known, Joshua. I'm very sad."

"Can you come to the restaurant sometime this week?" Ares asked. "It would be good to have you, to share memories a little. We'd feel more comfortable, there. Yes?"

"I would like that," I said.

"THIS ONE IS from when we were just starting out," Deo said. All of the customers had long since left, and he sat down in his chair and spoke slowly, with the relish of an experienced story-teller. "When the restaurant was still small, and your father was working his way through school. We were just a little Athena then. Right?" He looked at his brother.

"From when the restaurant was still up on Park," Ares said. Shorter than Deo, Ares had the same small, dark, intelligent eyes. They were like identical teddy bears in two different sizes. "There used to be a man who owned most of Montreal. Everything, he built everything. When the city was still growing, he would buy houses at the edge of the city and turn them into bigger houses, offices. Then Montreal would grow and he would own a piece of downtown. Downtown properties. These he would sell, and then buy new houses, farther out, doing the same thing again. It was a good plan, you know, in a city on the rise. He still owns a few of them."

"That's right," Deo said. "He still owns. Place Desjardins, down at the bottom of Guy? He owns that building there, with the green sparkles. Or his wife does, he's passed away now."

"Jean LaRoche?" I said. From where I sat I could see past the two of them, out the window and onto Guy. It had rained earlier, and now the street lights' reflections sparkled in the pavement.

"That is right," Deo said. "Jean LaRoche, that is right." He shook a thick, approving finger at my face, then scooped at some baklava still left on the dessert tray. "Jean LaRoche used to come to Athena every day. Every single day. He would have fish and fried zucchini."

"And the wine," Ares came back holding some cigarettes and a fresh glass of port. He put the port before Deo and handed him a cigarette. He offered one to me, but I shook my head and he tossed it on the table.

"Not wine!" Deo dismissed his brother with a wave of his hand.

"Yes, you're right," Ares said. He lit his cigarette and then leaned over to light Deo's. "It was Dom Perignon, the champagne of royalty. Perfect for Mr. LaRoche, the king of Montreal. Every day he used to come in, and he would usually bring his wife with him. You didn't mention that, Deo." Ares paused for a drag, then continued. "Even though he worked so hard, he would make a point of breaking every day to bring his wife here. And she would feed him. She would cut up the zucchini and fish into tiny little bites, and stack them on top of each other, and feed him these perfect little mouthfuls." He demonstrated on the tabletop, covered now with crumbs and fish bones, rubbing his fingers against one another in a cutting motion. "And the two of them would drink the Dom Perignon together."

"Just one glass each," Deo added. "He was old, she was old, so only one glass. They just loved the champagne with their meal, a little luxury they allowed themselves, but they weren't getting drunk. It was lunchtime, you know. And then Mr. LaRoche would say, 'The rest for the boys,' and send it back into the kitchen, for me and whoever else was in there."

"Deo drank Dom Perignon almost every day," Ares said. "For what, six years?" The younger brother was more relaxed than Deo. But there was a quality about him, something in his pressed shirts and dry handshakes made it easy to feel at home in his presence. He excelled at that — knowing his customers' names, remembering what they ordered on their last visit, the subtle suggestion that you were not like everyone else who came through his door. He was a restaurateur in the classical sense.

"More than that. More than six years. Eight years? Yes, eight or nine years. And your father was his favourite. He would always ask for your father to serve them. They would talk about simple things: the hockey, the weather, books. But he loved him. If he were still alive, he would be very sad to hear of what's happened." Deo sighed and pulled a hand through his greasy beard. Outweighing his brother by at least a hundred pounds, he was a man of books and food. In the kitchen, with a fresh fish and a hot pan before him, his talents were unmatched. "He is an easy man to befriend, your father," Deo said. I smiled at him, and he blushed a little, perhaps ashamed of his sudden sentimentality. "Anyway, the story."

"Yes. Okay." Ares spread his hands a little and shook his head. He always seemed to be apologizing for Deo. "Jean LaRoche was very rich, perhaps the richest man in Canada at the time. There were many wealthy men in Canada then, when the dollar was still worth something. Mr. LaRoche was likely the king of the kings, though. Surpassingly rich, he was above even men like Eaton, Thor, Peterson. Do you know those names?"

Deo leaned over and waved his hand vigorously in the middle of the table. "A billion," he said. "He probably had a billion dollars."

"Easily a billion," Ares said. "Anyway, one day Mr. LaRoche was in here for lunch, and as he finished, while he and his wife were preparing to leave, he said to your father, 'Harold, do you boys like horses?' Your father went to the track fairly often, and Deo and I grew up on a stable, so he said, 'Yes, yes, of course.' Mr. LaRoche took his hand and said, 'Then you meet me tomorrow morning at Dorval.' And then he left."

"The next day we closed the restaurant and drove out to Dorval, Deo and I and your father," Ares said, taking over again. "Mr. LaRoche was waiting for us, and he took us outside, and do you know what was there?"

I waited.

"His plane!" Deo said. "His own plane!"

Ares chuckled at his brother's excitement.

"This really was his own personal plane. His name was written along the side in bright red. LaRoche. We were amazed. And he flew us to Toronto."

"The ties, Ares," Deo said. "You forget the ties!" He laid an elbow on the table and gripped my shoulder. "When we get on the plane, Mr. LaRoche says to us, 'Boys, if you're going to fly on my plane, you must do me one thing.' So we say, 'Anything, Mr. LaRoche.' We would have done anything, we were crazy for this. And he says, 'Boys, you must wear my colours.' He takes out these three ties, red and gold striped, and he puts them on us. They were silk ties, I still have them. This, I felt, this is right, when I put that tie on."

"That's true," Ares said. "He did give us the ties. I don't know where mine is."

"In the office. Mine is in the office, with the books. I bet yours is in the office too, Ares."

"Maybe," Ares nodded. "Have you seen that tie, your father's?"

"I just saw it today," I said. I had been cleaning out my father's closet, organizing and putting some older items together for consignment. The tie had been among these, a fraying silk that was an antique compared to his others.

"Good," Deo said. "Keep it. Don't lose that tie."

"Right," Ares said. "So when we got to the racetrack in Mississauga, we had these ties on that let everyone know we were distinguished guests of Mr. LaRoche. The racing scene was huge then. It isn't so popular anymore, but at that time it was still a big thing. And it was the first of July, the Canada Day race. Imagine our version of the big races they do in the United States. This was like that, a Canadian Kentucky Derby. And the three of us were guests of honour."

"To see his horse. What a horse." Deo was slumping slightly in his seat, but he brought a kind of dignity to his streaked apron and sagging white pants. "Bucephalus. The horse of Alexander the Great, tamed by being turned toward the sun. Bucephalus." He rolled the word around in his mouth like a hard candy.

"That's right," Ares said. "Mr. LaRoche's horse was named Bucephalus. 'Do you want to come see it?' he asked us, and we went down to the backstretch. Of course, this was early, several hours before the race, so it was only us in the stable. The horse, you can imagine, was something else."

"It was fucking magnificent," Deo said. "Like a woman, a beautiful woman. It was a male horse, but, you know, we're from Greece, we know beautiful women. And this horse was like a woman. So powerful, so strong. It stood so proudly. As if it knew, from its legs to its mane, that it was a creature of God."

"I've never seen another like it," Ares said. "LaRoche went off to find the trainer, and left us there alone with this horse. We knew how to handle it ... we even had a horse of our own here in Montreal for a while, one we ran out in Lachine. We knew perfectly well how to handle a horse. I got down, just to check its legs, and I spoke to it for a minute, whispering. It was such a lovely animal, I really can't even explain. Suddenly, this woman appeared. A very proper woman, with a pink sundress on. A big hat too. She said to us, 'Is this your horse, boys?' Not accusing at all. I said, 'Yes, Ma'am, he's going to run a fine race today.' And the lady smiled. 'He looks that he will,' she said. Then she came closer, and stood nearby for a minute and smiled again, and then left. She had absolutely no doubt that the horse belonged to us. After she had gone, your father told us that she was Jackie Onassis."

"That's right," Deo said quietly, under his breath, "I had almost forgotten." He sounded strangely apologetic. Outside, through the window, I saw a couple stagger into the middle of the road. A blonde girl, early twenties, was helping her boyfriend along to somewhere, likely home. He had his arms around her and she was dragging him like a sleigh, laughing as the wind blew her hair up around her head. His face rested on her shoulder, and he kissed her cheek over and over as they moved slowly forwards.

"After that we met up with Mr. LaRoche and walked back out, across the track, heading toward the grandstand. As we were walking, though, we heard these voices from the bleachers. *Hey, pretty boys, how did the horse cock taste? Hey, assholes, make sure you're pretty enough for the show!*"

"We didn't know what this was!" Deo exclaimed. "We looked at Mr. LaRoche, we thought, you know, he'd be terrified. They were screaming right at us! But then we realize, oh, they are screaming in Greek! They are just some fans in the stands, they don't know us at all! Some idiots. And then, right in front of them, we went up to the trustees' lounge."

"Yes," Ares said, "we get to the elevator that takes you to the grandstand from the track, and we get in, and the boy in the elevator nods at Mr. LaRoche, and we go up. And up. And up. I figured when we went past the grandstand we'd stop at the fifth floor, where the owners' boxes are. But we kept going up, to the sixth floor, the trustees' lounge."

"This place, you wouldn't believe it," Deo jumped up from his chair. It fell over behind him, but he was too excited to notice. "We take off our jackets in the coatroom, and the coats there … the furs! Mink, otter, fox! Some others I didn't even know. And it was the summer! They were too rich for the heat! I tell you, if I just —"

"There were people there too, the kinds of people you only see in the newspaper." Deo picked up his chair and sat down and Ares resumed.

"The Eatons were there, they had a horse."

"You know how the crowds at these things work," Deo gestured in the air as he explained. "All the waspies together, mostly around the Eatons. Right? All the old whites. And then, by the door, a Greek, who saw us and smiled. Mister Onassis himself, there with his princess, although they did not look happy together. He would die the year afterwards, he was already very sick. A Jew, too, Jacob Lapinsky. They stood away from the others; you could see they had been doing some proper drinking. Who else, Ares?"

"Who else?" Ares stroked his bare chin as he considered the question. "Maurice Richard was there. Guy Lafleur. Pierre Trudeau was there. And the women. I don't even need to tell you about the women, I bet. You know the kind of women at these things.

First-class beauties, in designer dresses with whole jewellery stores around their necks."

Deo grunted and drummed his fingers on his chest.

"The food," he said. "Tell him about the food, Ares."

"The food was incredible. Caviar, filet mignon, all the things you would expe —"

"The prawns!" Deo jumped up again, this time with such ferocity that he bumped the edge of the table, and I had to grab it to keep it steady. "You know the kinds of prawns! The prawns were so big, I've never seen. I mean, we're a fish restaurant. I go to the fish market every day. Still, I've never seen prawns so big as these." He held his two forefingers out, end to end. "Huge! I thought they were lobsters when I first saw them. Oh!" He wiped the back of his hand over his eyes, frustrated that he could not fully convey his excitement. "I tell you, fuck, I tell you," and he fell back into his chair.

"Yes," Ares said. "The food really was wonderful." He paused for a moment, as if paying his respects. They were restaurateurs, after all. "No one looked at us as outsiders, though. Not one person even began to question what Deo and I were doing there. Except, well … I went to one of the waitresses who had a cigarette tray, and I said, 'Excuse me, how much are those cigarettes?' She gave me this look, very charmingly, but like I had told her some dirty secret about myself. She said to me, 'No one here pays for anything.' And then she gave me a pack of cigarettes!"

"I'm going to get some prawns," Deo announced, and he stood up, left the table and went to the kitchen. Outside the window, a police car flew by, its lights blazing but its wail muted by the other sounds of the city.

"I suppose they knew from how we bet on the races too," Ares said. "Mr. LaRoche came to us at the end of the day, as the stakes were getting higher and the big race was coming up, and he said to your father, 'Harold, tell me who's going to win it.' We had the program with us, and your father was making a big deal of the handicapping. Finally he said, 'Well, Mr. LaRoche, it makes me sorry to say it, but I pick Bucephalus to come second, and Brushstroke to win.' There was this one horse, Brushstroke. We had seen him when we were down in the paddock, and he was ... he hypnotized your father and me. He didn't have the presence Mr. LaRoche's horse had, not the same kind of grace at all. But there was energy around him, so thick it was like he was wearing armour. This horse was a monster. A legend, there on the field." Ares finished his cigarette and used it to light the one left on the table earlier.

"Mr. LaRoche said to your father, 'Okay, we'll bet that to win.' Then we went to the betting wicket, and the old man bets four dollars on Brushstroke to win and Bucephalus to place. Four dollars! I saw, when he opened his wallet, that those four bills was all the cash he had. Yet here at the restaurant he only ever paid us in hundreds. But who needs money in a place where everyone has so much? After he finished, I made my own bet. A hundred dollars, at seven to one, on Brushstroke."

Deo came back with a plate of a dozen shrimp, bright pink and plump. "They were the size of three of these," he said as he set them down. He popped one wet slug in his mouth, then rinsed it down with the rest of his port.

"So," Ares said, "the four of us watched the horses get loaded in. We sat with Mr. LaRoche and this other ancient, funny little gentleman. He had a lime-green coat on, and a very small head. He was shrinking in his old age, and in this lime coat with its great shoulder pads, he was maybe trying to retain some of his size. I thought he might have been one of the old jockeys. I was afraid

Deo would step on him and never notice! Anyway, Mr. LaRoche introduced him ... what was his name, Deo?"

"Dreyfus. Archie Dreyfus. I'll never forget that. He was so animated, like a little boy. He stood up to shake our hands."

"Right, Dreyfus. So Mr. Dreyfus, we soon learned, was the owner of Brushstroke, and he was overjoyed that I had bet on his horse. For some reason, he considered your father's advice to be a guarantee of victory. 'You boys look to know what you're talking about,' he said. Everyone there called us boys, even though we must have been ... I don't know, in our mid-thirties at the time."

"When was it?" I asked.

"Seventy-four," Deo said, and Ares nodded.

"Twenty-seven," I said. "My father, at least."

"Right," Deo said. He exchanged a look with Ares. "So we were a few years more than that, early thirties." There was a pause, as if everyone felt someone else should be the next to speak. Finally, Ares continued.

"Anyway, the race began, bang. All these old men leaned forward. The whole room went silent as everyone pressed against the window that looked out over the track."

"Except Dreyfus!" Deo spoke in a wonder-infused whisper. "He stands, and he pretends to ride. 'Yes! Yes! Yes!' he screams, and he shakes his hands like he has reins in them, and he shakes his tiny old man's ass, and no one says anything." Deo's voice had gradually been growing louder, and suddenly he took off around the room, heaving his drunken body into a horse shuffle, holding his hands before him and bobbing his head. "Just like that," he said.

"It was just like that," Ares agreed. "The race had begun, and right away it was between only Brushstroke and Bucephalus. There were some legendary horses in that race. Appearance Fee, he went on to win every big Canadian race the next year. Half a Hero, he was a real avenger, he won some important races too. Pulled Straight, an American-owned horse, he was a stallion, he looked like something out of *Black Beauty*. This, though, this was a war waged between just two. They pulled ahead going around the first turn, it was like the other horses hung back to watch them, and after that it was something: always shoulder to shoulder, their big great pounding bulks throwing up the dirt behind them, and the thunder of their hooves. It was a moving thing. They knew they were alone, too, pit solely against one another, and they danced together, trading the lead around the length of the track, testing themselves a little, and then into the final turn Brushstroke just summoned something. It was a speed like magic, it was really ..."

"Destiny, Ares." Deo had sat down again, quietly, and rested his chin in his hands. "It was destiny."

"Maybe. Maybe you're right, Deo. Whatever sparked him, it was sublime, a thing most men never have the privilege of seeing. Bucephalus was just left behind, as if he suddenly surrendered, and Brushstroke went out alone into the track and over the line. You couldn't see another horse behind him when he finished." Ares paused and glanced toward Deo.

"And then he broke," Ares said.

"You know when a boy on a bike hits something, and he flies forward over the handlebars?" Deo said. "It was like that. He just stopped, without slowing down. Legs buckled and slumped — *shumpf* — forward and down. The jockey flew up off him maybe twenty feet, broke both his arms."

"Mr. Dreyfus was right behind us," Ares said. "Jumping and kicking at the win, and when he saw that ... a sound came out of him, a child's cry ... you don't expect those kinds of sounds from old men. It was as if they'd torn his throat right out through his mouth. No one had paid him any attention, when he was leaping around, but now they all turned. They couldn't bear to watch what was on the track."

"The horse was dead. Dropped right dead. I've never seen the life go from something so fast." Deo leaned back in his chair.

"Mr. Dreyfus," Ares said, "he just put his hands over his eyes and cried. No one would say anything to him, because none of them knew what to say. They were men of business, old men of steel and oil and empires, and they didn't know how to deal with their friend in tears. But I went up to him — Deo will remember it — I went up to him and put my arms around him, in his tiny lime-green jacket. And he laid his head on my shoulder, and he cried. For a long time. An old man like that, and he just cried!"

"Of course," Deo said after a minute, "it was only on the plane ride home that this fool remembered he had won seven-hundred dollars."

"That's right," Ares said. "I never got it."

This wasn't the whole truth, as I'm sure they knew I was aware. Dreyfus had given the money to my father, who spent it on my mother's plane ticket to join him in Canada. The winnings from that race had funded the creation of my family.

I ASKED ARES for one of his cigarettes, and moved chairs so that he and I could share an ashtray. From my new seat, I faced the wall instead of the window. Deo had taken up painting as a hobby, and the dark wooden panels were decorated with several of his canvasses. The largest one was an endless swirl of blues and greens, complex yet beautiful. It struck me how, for the past few hours, the view enjoyed by my father's best friends had been so different from my own.

INDIGENOUS BEASTS

THE FIRST TIME I saw Ray again was when my husband, George, and I moved back to Toronto. George had said it was important to invite him over right away, to show that there were no hard feelings.

"We're going to need friends here," George said when I suggested maybe it wasn't such a good idea, given the history Ray and I had. "He used to be a friend to both of us; he should be again."

So Ray came over that night, our second in the new apartment. It was January, a messy time for a move, and the floors were still dirty from the slush on the movers' boots.

"I MEAN, New York was great, but I just didn't see an opportunity for anything amazing in it. Sure, I was taken care of, and it was secure, but you know? I thought taking a chance was worth it, for the potential reward. Here I could be a partner before I'm thirty." George was explaining why we had come back to Toronto.

"Definitely, yeah," Ray said.

We were in what would eventually become the living room,

drinking vodka and pineapple juice. I was sitting on the floor, while the two of them sat on the boxes that had arrived that day. Ray was sitting on "Ski Stuff."

We had all grown up together in Mississauga. We weren't really friends until our senior year of high school, when we shared an English class. After graduation George left to study at Queen's, and Ray and I started dating.

"So, what about you? I'll say it again, man, you look great." George gives compliments very easily. That's what makes him a good lawyer, I think. He knows how to make someone feel comfortable.

"Yeah, thanks," Ray said. "I joined a gym and they have a tanning thing there, makes you look like a lifeguard all year." I looked closely at him. The skin around his eyes was pale in comparison to the rest of his face.

Ray and I had dated for almost a year, and then his sister died of leukemia. He used to blame me for keeping him away from her while she was sick, although really he used me as an excuse. Whenever he went to visit her he would come back complaining, describing the sour smell of sickness that permeated her room and how everyone treated her like she was already dead. Then he would take me to bed and be rough with me in a way I sometimes enjoyed and sometimes felt used by, like I was a vessel more than a lover.

Eventually I told him to get out of the relationship if it was so much trouble, and when he didn't I took matters into my own hands, moving to New York for acting school. He sent me letters, thick envelopes with "Please Read Me" written on their backs like props from an *Alice in Wonderland* movie, but I didn't open them, and eventually they stopped. One night, drunk after a cast party, I pulled them out from under my bed and threw them over the balcony of my apartment, into the street. I regretted this the next day, but they were gone and there was nothing I could do about it.

I was in New York for three years before George arrived on the promise of a fat salary from one of the big Manhattan firms. Our friendship flared into romance quickly, and he proposed to me that July, on a horse ride in Central Park. I knew it was coming because people don't seem to take hansom cabs for any other reason, but he was so sincere about it that I feigned surprise.

George and I were a good team, the kind of husband and wife who very effectively navigate through the day-to-day. He treated me very well. We never talked about Ray directly, but sometimes in bed George would ask if he was the best lover I'd ever had, and I knew whom he was comparing himself to. I always said yes, yes, of course, without hesitation.

"The girls in your class must love you," I said. Ray taught Social Studies at a prestigious private high school uptown. He did look good, but in a funny, overstyled way, like he had bought his outfit — black blazer, crisp white shirt, jeans — just for that evening. He was bigger than I remembered; his frame wasn't as sharp and bony as it used to be, but still skinny. He still had fine, long hair, and it kept falling over his eyes.

"Yeah, I do get a poem now and then, actually," Ray laughed. "But everyone else on the staff has at least a hundred years on me, so I'm kind of the pick of a poor litter."

"How did you get into teaching anyway?" George asked. He pulled out a new pack of cigarettes and began scratching at the plastic wrap. He had only recently started smoking again, and was still self-conscious about falling back into the habit. "I don't ever remember you having much interest in class while we were in school."

"Yeah, you're right," Ray said. "I hated this stuff the first time round."

George opened the cigarettes and offered the pack to Ray, who took one.

"After I got back from New Zealand, it was the only thing I got accepted for at the college. They put a premium on my 'life experience,' they said. I guess I'm just lucky that I ended up enjoying it so much. I'm good at it, I think."

"New Zealand? How long were you there?" I said. There were three things I had never told George about Ray. The first was the letters. The second was that he had a sense of adventure that, especially in those days after high school, I had found irresistible.

"Almost three years. I was down by Southland, in the country-side." He paused to let George light his cigarette.

"What did you do there?" I said. He laughed.

"It's kind of funny, actually. Do you know what sheep inverting is?"

"No idea, but it sounds dirty." George only made jokes about what other people were saying, something I didn't notice until we began living together. It was like he didn't have any stories of his own. Ray smiled at him.

"Not really. Actually, it's pretty basic ... just, very ... unusual. Sheep are big business there. Wool comes in different consistencies, and the best wool for shearing is along the back — especially in Leicesters, the kind of sheep I inverted. So farmers breed the sheep with the broadest backs possible. Over time, this has made the little bastards almost triangle shaped, with carriages that dwarf their legs. They look like those weightlifters you see on TSN late at night." He ran a hand through his hair. "Anyway, this causes a very simple problem. New Zealand is covered with hills, right? The sheep are going up and down hillsides all day, and they fall over. The problem is, because their legs are so pathetic compared to the rest of their bodies, they aren't strong enough to get themselves back up."

NATHAN SELLYN

80

"So your job was to flip them back over?" I said. I pulled an ice cube out of my empty glass and sucked on it.

"Exactly. I went around all day on an ATV, looking for sheep that had gotten laid out. When I found one, I'd get off and flip him over. It seems stupid, but it's absolutely necessary. Those sheep are expensive, and if one gets left alone like that he'll die for sure. So breeders hire one or two guys, depending on the size of their herd, to be sheep inverters. That's the proper name they've given it. The guy I worked with had been doing it for almost forty years."

"Jesus," George said. "Can you imagine that being your career?" He shook his head and glanced at me. The wall behind him was bare and spotty from the furniture of the previous owners. Eventually, in an effort to cheer ourselves up during the winter, we would paint the room lime green.

"Yeah, no shit." Ray ashed his cigarette into his empty glass, then realized this maybe wasn't appropriate behaviour for a guest. He looked over at me guiltily.

"It's fine," I said, and smiled at him to show I wasn't just being polite. He smiled back at me and shrugged, which instantly lent his face an impish, boylike quality. The third thing I had never told George about Ray was that he made me feel the same kind of sexy I felt onstage, like I was the only person in the room worth paying attention to.

"Is that why you came back?" I asked.

"Kind of," he said. "Well, not really. I mean, it didn't pay much, but it was enough. I definitely could have seen myself doing it for a while longer. Outside in the sun all day? No thinking? I could just get high and drive around. It was, actually, perfect for the kind of guy I was back then."

"So what happened? Why'd you come home?" George asked.

He leaned forward and put his elbows on his knees. It was a great impression of someone who was paying attention.

"Actually," Ray said. "It's funny, but I can tell you the one thing that got me around to leaving. One morning I went out into a total downpour. It doesn't rain very often in New Zealand, but when it does it's a shitstorm, you know?" He moved one hand as he spoke, emphasizing syllables with a fist. "This one morning I go out and it's just pissing, I can't see more than ten feet in front of me. I cruise with the herd for a while, and then I start finding stragglers. I don't know if the rain had made the ground slippery or what, but they were all over the place. Little dark spots on the edge of the group was how I saw them. Dark, then white when I came close. White and wet and bleating. They make a hell of a noise when they're on their backs; I used to be able to do a really good imitation of it." He cleared his throat and made a sound like the first note in a fire siren, his face going red from the effort. The ice cube flew from my mouth as I burst out laughing. I could feel both of them staring at me, Ray in appreciation and George in bewilderment, since it's usually tough to get me to do more than giggle.

"Yeah, guess I don't do it too well anymore," Ray said. "Anyway, they were falling like fucking crazy. It seemed like for every one I got up, two more fell down. I almost thought about herding them into the barn for the day, figured they could skip eating to stay alive. Didn't though, mainly because it wasn't my choice. My boss there, an old guy called Culver, would've killed me." George grabbed the bottle of vodka from the floor and refilled his drink.

"The sheep just kept tumbling. After an hour or so, I was fucking exhausted. But it seemed like I'd gotten them all up. Part of the problem had been that they were on a hillside, and the steep patches send them over every time. But I'd gotten them off that, onto a little plain, and I thought things were fine. But I could hear this one bleat, coming from out in the rain, and I knew, from counting, that we were one short. So I drove in circles from the group, going a little wider every time, looking for this one bugger of a goddamn sheep." There was a crackle from outside that sounded like fireworks, and then some yelling. We had moved into a good neighbourhood, but not a great one.

George glanced toward the window. "Jesus," he said. "I wonder what that's about." He looked at his watch. "More importantly, I wonder when the food is coming." We had ordered Chinese when Ray arrived. Our pantry at that point consisted of whatever take-out menus were tacked to the fridge.

"Yeah," I said, "it's been almost an hour, babe. Should I call and check on it?"

"We'll give it another ten minutes. Ray, you finish." George pulled out two more cigarettes, but Ray shook his head.

"I'm fine without another, thanks. Trying to quit, actually. It's the worst thing when you're a teacher."

"Tell him it's the worst thing, period." I said.

"I'd be lying."

"Exactly," George said. There was an uncomfortable pause in the conversation.

"Please," I said after a moment. "Tell us the rest."

"Right. So I drive around looking for this sheep forever. I can hear it bleating, but the rain is coming down so hard I can't keep track of the direction very well. Then, finally, I find him, right against the fence. A young ram, still growing. Probably about a hundred fifty, hundred sixty pounds. He was behind a rock, that's why I hadn't seen him before. Anyway, he's over on his side, and now that I've found him I can see why he was making so much racket.

There's blood all along his coat, he's practically swimming it. So I slide my arms under him to flip him and get a better look, but just when I start to lift I see his stomach is totally opened up. The bastard had run himself right into the barbwire fencing, and it tore him open. His intestines were all pooled beneath him. He was lying on his own guts."

"Fucking hell," George said. He was almost through the second drink.

I put my hand over my mouth.

"Yeah, it was terrible. I mean, I saw them slaughter the sheep all the time, so the blood and stuff didn't really get to me, you know? But the sound he was making, Christ. I could only imagine what it would be like, to not only be split right damn open, but then be squashing your own guts."

"So what did you do?" I asked.

Ray shrugged. "I killed him."

A police car wailed by outside, and we all paused to let it pass.

"I figured it was what I'd want. They never really trained us for that situation, and I couldn't just leave him. So I lined my little four-wheeler right up against his head, then hit the gas. I just tried not to look down. Culver went out with the truck and got him later that evening, after the rain had stopped."

"Fucking hell," George said again. I glared at him. I wanted him to be quiet for a minute. Ray waited until I turned back to him before continuing.

"Anyway, after that, I just didn't enjoy being out there as much. I felt bad around the sheep. Not that I was guilty or anything. Just, it was more ... I don't know, something just told me it was time to come home."

"Amen," George said.

WHEN RAY LEFT, George shook his hand and I kissed him on the cheek. But when George, now several drinks in, went clumsily back to the business of unpacking, I stayed by the window to watch Ray climb tentatively down the icy steps to his car. He stopped at the driver door and looked back up toward our apartment, but if he could see me he didn't let on.

"Come on, babe," George said from behind me. "Get into bed and we'll make something worthwhile of tonight."

But I ignored him, staying by the window until Ray pulled away, trying to remember the details of the memories I'd made with him. I was still trying to remember them an hour later, when George and I climbed into our sheetless new bed for only the second time. I pressed close against him. Canada was colder than I remembered.

YOU WANT TO WIN

I WAS RETURNING two plants the day I saw a man kill himself in the bathroom fixtures aisle at Home Depot. It hadn't gone well, for me or for him.

The guy at the return counter had bulging, purple bags beneath his eyes. He wouldn't take the plants, asparagus ferns.

"What happened to these, son?" he said, running his hands over them.

"I don't know," I said. "Just weren't very green anymore. I've got a receipt."

"Our policy is for plants that die on their own," he said. "You killed these. They haven't been watered in weeks."

"What?" I said. I'd watered them once, the day I brought them home. I had been looking for something to brighten up the sterile basement suite I was living in.

"Water is food for a plant. That's what it eats." I felt my face growing hot. "You think you could go two months without food? These things were at the healthiest points in their lives, and you killed 'em." He pushed the plants toward me, disgusted, and moved to another customer.

I stared after him for a moment, then turned away with a snort. I found the healthy ferns at the back of the store and, when no one was looking, shoved mine in alongside them. They made an eyesore of the display. These are our every day revenges.

I passed the guy as I was leaving. He was older, around fifty, wearing thick glasses and a red track suit. I saw him pull it from his pocket — a revolver. Slipped it in his mouth and pulled. No hesitation. That struck me, later. I'd need a moment, for sure. Or maybe he had been hesitating, thinking about it all morning. Maybe he'd been drifting around Home Depot, looking at carpet swatches and washer-dryer combinations and building up the strength. Luckily his eyes were closed, or we would have been looking right at each other. What would have happened then? Would he have gotten stage fright?

The bullet came out the back of his head in a spray of gore, shattering a sink several feet behind him. The blood was darker than blood from cuts and scrapes, almost purple. And grey, hunks of grey. Yogurt. That's the best description. It looked like someone had blown apart a carton of raspberry yogurt. I took the scene in and then looked away, just stared at one of the faucets that lay between his corpse and me. Gold, with a glass knob; it wasn't touched. Ten feet away, behind him, everything was painted by the gore. But in the space between us, the world remained shrink-wrapped and quality-guaranteed, untouched. Then I felt hands on my shoulders, and an orange vest dragged me aside. I turned and vomited over the key-cutting machine.

IN THE AFTERNOON I went to pick up my friend Elvin for work. He came jerkily out of his little bungalow, pausing to slowly ease the front door closed. The way he glanced back as he came around the car told me Claire was awake. He tumbled in, a goofy grin splitting his little head, slammed the door and lit a cigarette.

"Rough morning, buddy?" I pulled the car back out. Elvin lived right by the highway; you could see the overpass from his front window. I'd been picking him up since I started working at the mill. It wasn't employment to be proud of, just feeding sticks through a wood stripper for eight hours with a bunch of guys who had never finished high school, but it paid great thanks to the union. Over twenty bucks an hour. Elvin had known my older brother when they were younger, and he'd helped me land the mill job on the condition that I'd drive him in every day.

"Nah, nothing worse than the usual." He leaned down to tie up his boots, a pair of black hikers I'd given him for Christmas. They were a real nice pair, Timberlands. "I couldn't find my belt, and Claire started on about how I'd probably left it at some girl's place. Kidding around though, just getting angry so I'd get out on time and all." Elvin fucked up tying his left boot and started again.

"Find it?" I sped up and merged onto the highway. There was a red smear in the merge lane, probably from roadkill. I wondered why I had never noticed it before, whether this morning had changed me somehow. I put my hand in my pocket, over the business card a cop had given me. Call me if you remember anything, he'd said. I told him there wasn't much I was going to forget.

"Huh?" Elvin picked something out of his ear and wiped it along the inside of the car door.

"Where was the belt?"

"Oh. Fuck, that's the funny thing. In my pants." He reached into his pocket and pulled out a small glass pipe.

"Goddamn, Elvin, come on." He had a few years on me,

twenty-nine with a kid, and the man was getting stoned at two-thirty in the afternoon.

"What? What? You got a problem with this today?" He shook his head and took a hit, then blew it out the window. My hands started tapping on the wheel. "You want me to put the radio on?" He leaned over and pushed the volume knob.

We drove for the first side of my Stones mix, me with my hands at ten and two and Elvin just leaning back, eyes half closed, smiling and humming along. It was a nice day, one of the first that spring without rain, and he left the window open a little. The best weather for driving, when the air is clean and you're warm as long as you stay in the sun.

"Elvin, I saw a man shoot himself today." The words came out fast, like I'd vomited again. But he didn't hear me. I could see his head bobbing out the corner of my eye, a second behind the music. "Elvin."

"Yessir?" He sat up straight, as if coming out of a dream. I nudged the volume down.

"I saw a guy shoot himself at Home Depot this morning." It was easier the second time.

"What the fuck were you doing at Home Depot?"

"Returning those plants, the ferns. He killed himself, man." Elvin let out a long whistle, one note.

"Messy?" he said.

"Yeah, I threw up. Never seen anything like that before, man."

Elvin nodded, then ran a hand through his hair. "Jesus. That's fucked up. Fucked right up, Nealy. I mean, I ain't ever seen anything like that either. Seen men killed, sure, or a man, but it was a car accident. And I've seen men beat up pretty bad. But never seen a man gun himself down, though. Jesus, that takes some balls."

Elvin always spoke as though each thought had exploded out of the period in the sentence before it. They weren't impressive thoughts, for the most part, but they fell over each other to get out.

"In a fucking hardware store, too. Fucking Home Depot." I glanced away from the road to see his expression. He was either legitimately shaken or doing his best impression of someone who was.

"Yeah," I said. "Yeah. I can't even imagine doing something like that. Doing that kind of violence to yourself." We were behind a school bus. The kids had their faces pressed against the window. They were pointing at Elvin and laughing. He gave them the finger and they jumped back behind the seats.

"Yeah, it's fucked up. Sorry, man, I didn't know you'd been through that. Real fucked up. Especially for you, way out of your league." Elvin always liked to hint at how he felt I'd had life easy. He was harder than me, I'll admit it. Everyone at the mill was. Most of them would bang a paraplegic and then make her walk home. I stayed quiet, didn't defend myself. The tape switched sides and we sat without talking for a few minutes more.

"What's the roughest thing you've ever seen before that?" He said it like a challenge.

"I don't know." I think Elvin had noticed that my hands were shaking. Not quivering, either, but shaking properly, flopping around from the wrist like I'd jammed my fingers in a socket.

"I'm just talking with ya, Nealy. What is it? Must be something. I know your brother's got guns. You never seen him shoot something up? Fuck, that dog your mum has is begging to get shot."

I didn't say anything.

"I know you got one, Nealy."

"I don't know," I said again.

"Bullshit, man, come on, tell me something."

"Tell you what?" I pulled off the highway into an Esso. "I've got nothing like that, nothing like seeing a man blow his fucking head off, Elvin." I drove up beside a pump and slammed the door as I got out.

In fourth grade, I went to Bradley Lorent's birthday party. It was early September. Summer was ending and the days were long and sweaty. After cake we watched a Chucky movie, and the "Thriller" video, and then his brother came into the living room and told us all to go outside. His brother was about sixteen, and we were all nine or ten, so we listened. I didn't say a word. I could have, I think. If I'd wanted, I could have gone and hid somewhere, or just started crying right then, and I would have gotten out of it. But I didn't. When you're a kid, being older is an absolute, and so we all did as we were told.

He and two friends brought us out back, to the field behind Brad's house. It was full of wheat stiffs, or whatever you call them, yellow stalks that came up two or three feet off the ground. We could see across the wheat, see the dip and curve of the earth all the way across to the long, dark line of the forest.

The older boys — Ian, Forrest and Greg. Ian was one of my own brother's friends, so I kind of knew him, but he never acknowledged me. On the walk to the field, he kept licking his fingers and holding them above his head, trying to test the wind. He didn't have a shirt on, and his arms were tanned darker than his chest. Forrest was Bradley's brother. He had chunky black boots and a swagger to match. He called his father by his first name. And he had a motorcycle. Everyone knew about his motorcycle, and how on the same day he first brought it to the high school, the helmet around the back of his neck, he had fucked Kimberly Quinn in the PE office. Even your mother knew about

Forrest Forcan. And Greg, who I'd never seen before and wouldn't ever meet again.

The three of them lined us up, Bradley, six other kids, and me, and pulled out some slingshots. Not the kind you make from wood, but the real badass kind, the aluminum ones that brace against your wrist. Chris Chambers was beside me, whimpering into his chest. Chris' brother Colin was older, and held the town record for packs of cigarettes stolen from the gas station in one trip. Thirty-seven. Chris would eventually get busted trying to break that record.

"Here's the rules," Forrest looked at each of us while he talked, as if he was marshalling a children's army. We all stared back. I felt maybe a little privileged. "Y'all are going to get two minutes to hide out in the field. Then we're gonna come get you." Greg was pulling pea-sized metal lumps from his pocket and firing them into the earth with the slingshot. They stuck in where they hit. "If you cry, you're out. So don't cry, and you'll win. You want to win." He stopped suddenly, then turned around to whisper to Ian. Ian nodded, stuck two fingers in his mouth, and blew. Forrest smiled. "Go," he said.

We didn't move. No one even put a foot forward. I looked over at Bradley, but he was just staring back at his brother like everyone else. Then Ian jacked up his slingshot and fired a BB at a skinny blonde kid with a harelip, a family friend of Brad's none of us knew. It hit the kid in the shoulder and he went down in a heap, head between his knees. Somebody at the end of the line bolted into the field.

"Go, you shits!"

The rest of us took off, hands and legs flailing, diving into the wheat. The spiny tops tore at my cheeks as I plunged. I ran and ran, trying to put the war cries of the older boys behind me.

The wheat all looked the same, I couldn't tell how far I'd gone, but I barrelled on, holding my arms before me to stop the stiffs from snapping back against my face. Finally, I tripped. There was barbwire on the ground, the last remnants of a broken fence, and it caught the top of my foot and sent me flying. The soil filled my mouth, choking me before I could scream. I held my breath, motionless, straining to hear them. But it seemed like their shouts were everywhere, coming at me from all directions. I closed my eyes and curled my knees to my chest, trying to melt into the field itself. It didn't work.

I don't know who it was that came up behind me, but I was crying already when he arrived. "You're fucked," he said once. The BB hit the back of my head. The pain was so sudden, so blinding, that it made me spit all the dirt from my mouth. I gagged. Then his hand was on the back of my neck, burning and clammy. "Get back to the house, you little shit." By the time I stood up, he was gone.

MY GLOVES FELL out of my pocket when I leaned over to push the pump in. They were lined with sheep's wool, the real stuff, which made work much easier. Elvin's hands were hard and callused because of his shitty gloves. They kept the slivers out, but not the roughness. My hands were still soft.

I'd been in junior college for four years before I took the mill job. I did all kinds of courses. Business Administration. Information Systems. Marketing. Introductions to Economics, Philosophy, and Computer Science. Every one, even the Commerce degree I eventually piled up enough credits for, was useless. No one wanted to hire a junior college kid for anything more than photocopying and cold calls, and jobs like those don't even pay your car insurance. I'd taken the mill job because I missed having money, simple as that. My mum had gotten on my case a few times about maybe being a bank teller, she had a friend who was an account manager and could get me in, but that still seemed pretty bottom of the pile to me. I told her I'd drop a résumé off and never did.

Besides, working at the mill made you part of a family. From the New West sex shops to the East Hastings crackhouses, the Granville clubs to the South Surrey strip malls, mill workers knew people. So, in at least one way, working at the mill wasn't a step back. It was more like changing lines on the highway. Different speed, same direction.

WHEN I GOT back in the car I could tell Elvin had been thinking about the hardware store. A focus he normally lacked had come into his bloodshot eyes; they were lit with the concentration of a carefully formulated thought.

"You know, it's not that fucked up."

"What?"

"Killing yourself." He turned around in his seat slightly to face me. "I mean, fuck, I'm not gonna do it. It's ditching out, if you ask me. There's no balls in that. But it's not so crazy. Think about it. Monkeys and bugs and shit, they never suicide. Nothing does, 'cept humans. Nobody but us decides to go and blow their brains out."

I wasn't sure if he was right about that, but he didn't pause long enough for me to interrupt. He was waving his hands around, pummelling the space between us.

"Animals don't commit suicide because they don't know any better, they're not smart enough. People are. And being the smartest means we know we can flick the switch ourselves. Don't you think if beavers or bugs or monkeys were as smart as us, they'd kill themselves every time? What's the point of it? What is the point of living a beaver's life? Building fucking dams all day and shitting in the fucking woods. Life isn't worth it for them, but they don't know any better." He exhaled slowly. "Not that crazy if you ask me, Nealy."

I wanted to tell him that putting a revolver in your mouth was as crazy as crazy gets. I wanted to tell him suicide was for the Wal-Mart manager whose hysterectomy-scarred wife just left him for an eighteen-year-old with a new Prelude. But I would only have been proving his point. Plus, that guy in Home Depot hadn't looked crazy. He'd looked like my dad at my high school graduation.

WORK THAT DAY was slow going. It was a scorcher of a night, and even around eleven I was still sweating hard enough that my flannel stuck to my back. In the summer it would get worse, hot enough that some guys even broke safety code and went shirtless. Elvin was working a little down the line from me, giving some long story about when he used to be a janitor at a rec centre. He was saying how some nights he would go out back and set fire to the dumpster, just to have someone to talk to when the fire department came. I asked him if they knew he was setting the fires on purpose.

"Yeah, no," he said. "I don't know. If they knew, they knew why, too." When I laughed he looked over at me and slipped a finger inside his mouth, then worked his thumb like a safety. He thought it was funny, but I glanced down. His other hand was still on a piece of wood, it had caught the leather of his glove, and it was slowly sliding toward the stripper. I shouted at him, not words, just everything that was in my mouth at the time. He looked down and pulled away — the stripper caught the edge of his glove and ripped it right off his hand, into a whirring blur of blades and razors.

"Christ, pal," I said. Elvin was silent. He held his hand up before his face and made a fist, then relaxed it.

"Close one, huh?" he said.

"No shit," I said. I pulled the switch that shut the conveyor off — you can't have a man working the line without gloves on. Some guys started yelling from farther down the line as the conveyor slowed.

"Guess I'm just lucky, huh?"

"Yeah," I said to him. "You've got a horseshoe up your butt."

At midnight, when we got off, I went to find Murray, our supervisor, and I told him I was quitting. He didn't ask why. Someone had told him about that morning, and he just gave me a pat on the back and wished me luck. I gave Elvin my gloves that night when I dropped him off.

The next day I could have slept until the afternoon if I wanted to. But I woke up early. I had things to do.

MA BELLE

I AM STARING at my reflection in the window of the Angrignon metro. Nothing looks good in the metro. It's the lights, cruel fluorescents. They make fair skin waxy, tan skin yellow. But I look good tonight, magazine-cover good. Hair slicked forward and pulled over, clean shaven, cologne burning. Three sprays: one on the neck, one up the shirt, and one down the shorts. You never know, right? Nothing looks good in the metro, except me. Still, turning my head I can see the acne scars on my cheeks and the chest hair advancing up past the beachhead of my shirt collar. Minor things. Manly flaws. At thirty-one, I should carry some of the glamour of age.

All that said, if bodies are cars, mine is a taxi, and it feels like I've been carrying a fat man in the back seat for the last decade. My hairline is going. My gumline is going. They're racing, really, to see who can make me look more like my father first. And the joke is, he's dead.

Car crash, two years ago. Wasn't drinking, though, so he's still a role model. My mother watched him go right through the windshield, then twelve feet through the air into the semi in front of them. Last thing went through his head was his ass type-deal. I don't miss him much — the last time I saw him was when I accidentally opened their bathroom door to find him, wet and wrinkled from the shower, wrestling furiously with his limp cock.

My mum, though — since he's been gone, she's pretty much headed out too. She occupies herself running knitting clubs and United Way fundraisers, dating men who live in places with names like Sunnydale Farm and Farmhold Homes and Homewinds Centre. Bingo on Monday after dinner and shitting your pants on Sunday. I'm paying her a visit tonight, our monthly dinner date. Once I force back her meatloaf and beans, she'll give me some cash: $900, more than twice my rent. But the cost of living is higher when you are, quite simply, not very good at it.

And I'm only getting worse. I've been noticing something lately, something that really lets me know I've turned the corner on my youth. It's not the hair in the drain or the throb behind my eyes whenever I'm out in the sun. This is something that worries me far more than any checklist of aches and pains.

I work at a gas station, have for a long time. It's a good job, and I live right upstairs, so everything about it suits me fine. I'm the manager, it's easy. But I remember when I was just starting, ten years ago or so, that I'd sometimes catch a look from a girl. Maybe a teenager in the back of a station wagon, her mother driving her to field hockey practice or violin lessons. Maybe a whole Jeep full of blondes on their way downtown. I'd fill them up, give them a smile, and sometimes, just for a second, one would look back over her shoulder to catch my eye. Thinking about it, you know? About me.

I never get those looks anymore, not even from the mothers.

That worries me, I'll be honest. Makes me wonder what kind of rough beast I've become.

THIRTEEN STOPS later and I'm at St. Laurent station. The wind is coming in low and hard; I have to stick close to the buildings to protect my hair. There's about half an hour to kill before I meet Ma, so I head toward my favourite neon lights. The sidewalks are bloated with French girls in tube tops and Lebanese boys in knock-off silk shirts, their black hair plastered with product. I walk against the flow, staring right into a thousand jaded eyes. Their minds are all on the destination, not the journey.

Down the throat of an alley, a crowd of the worst is gathered. You know the type: unshaven, hollows under their eyes, peeling lips, baseball caps. The kind who don't know how much better they could have it. I press against them, shouldering through flannel shirts and hockey jerseys.

Two mutts are rolling around on the pavement, thrashing against the alley walls as often as each other. The fight is all teeth and skittering hind legs, a countdown until the first leg snaps. Dirty hunks of hamburger lie on the ground, soiled trophies for the victor. The dogs are emaciated beyond belief; the only things more horrible than the ribs stretching their flesh to transparency are the numbers branded into their sides — 10 and 9.

"What are the numbers for?" I ask a shorter man beside me. "*#1 Pere*" is written on his baseball cap. He must be on his way to do some Christmas shopping for his darlings.

"They are old racing dogs," he says, "from Sept-Iles." His breath is disgusting. "You see the numbers? 10, like Lafleur, and 9, like Richard. From when we were lions!"

THERE'S PLENTY of time before going to see my mother, so I join a dance-club lineup that contains some especially liberal-looking young women. T-backs poke over low-rise jeans; blouses are unbuttoned at the navel. All the girls wear next to nothing these days. I'm not complaining, but it makes it tougher than ever to spot the kind of woman who won't mind waking up in a motel room beside someone whose name she reads from his wallet. Slut, these days, is a relative term.

The club turns out to be a rock joint, a rarity. Most of the discos these days play the same music as the strip clubs — rap and Top 40, the kind of stuff that kids in high school listen to until the lead singer rapes someone their age and gets hauled off to an eighteen-hole prison. This place is more my level, full of shadows and corners that I can tell are playing host to the dirty acts of dirty people. Above the bar are stuffed moose heads with red Christmas lights for eyes, and everyone is wearing black makeup. They're all a little angry, but no one is looking to fight.

I grab two beers and make my way to a table by the dance floor. It's made from the kind of wood they use for high-school desks, and covered with graffiti about some girl named Marie. I stare out at the dance floor. It's early in the evening, so it's still just the girls, waiting for their boyfriends to get drunk enough to join them. On my sliding scale, the majority of them would score high, at least sevens. They look naive, suburban girls in the city for a Friday night.

It's not long before I have company. Funny how the clubs with the least welcoming appearances often house the friendliest patrons.

"What do you think of this music?" My guest is French, but he knows I'm English. A black mop of hair hangs over his eyes, and his leather jacket stretches around his muscles like a ball bag.

"Pardon me?" I try hard to listen to what's playing. It's death metal of some sort, cut-your-wrists-and-eat-your-dog type stuff. I don't really follow music like I used too; my schedule of nothing is far too hectic.

"The song that is on," he says. "Do you like it?"

"Sure." I nod, pulling on my beer. Nodding is always safe.

"Me too. This is The Shudders. They are a new band, from America."

"Right."

"I like too The Arachnids. They are from Sweden. But they sound American. Everything is a little American, these days. They make all the celebrities, like a machine for famous people. They love them. They care so much about the careless, you know?"

I keep nodding, because he seems to want to keep talking, and start my second beer.

"You come from Le Tigre?" he says.

"Huh?"

"The club, from across the street. Yes?"

"No." It's nice to know that my first impression is one of a guy who frequents nudie bars. I look around for an excuse to leave.

"I have a question," the Frenchie says. I raise my bottle, motion for him to continue. "Where do they get the skin, for the tit surgeries? If a girl get very big tits ..." and here he holds out his hands to display what he means, cupping imaginary road pylons, "where do the skin come from? So much skin!"

I don't answer right away. There's a girl on the dance floor I'm trying to get a better look at. It seems as though her friends have abandoned her for the bar, and she's dancing by herself, finding a beat she can enjoy alone. Then I lean back to my new friend.

"I don't know," I say. "What if you go get massive breasts, double Ns or something, total watermelons?" I mimic his illusion of breasts with my own hands. "What if you do that, get Guinness Record tits, and then some other girl goes out the next day and gets bigger ones, double Ts? How must that feel, to have tits so big you can't even stand up, and be nothing more than second best?" The Frenchie looks confused; he grins like an idiot. Perhaps he's hitting on me. He's more attractive than half the woman I've slept with.

The girl finds a beat, lashes out wildly with her hands, kicks her legs violently. She collides with some other dancers, a group of girls, who laugh at her and back away. She doesn't notice, or doesn't care, keeps shaking it alone. The Frenchie and I watch for a moment, appreciating her together.

"So, my friend," he finally says. "Do you maybe want some hash?" And there it is, his friendship explained away in a question.

"No," I say, "I don't." I kind of do, actually, but not his. I've got plenty of soft drugs at home to enhance evenings alone with the television, and under the table at a bar from someone you've never met is generally a poor way to buy drugs. Unfortunately, I've never been good at saying no.

"Wait," I say, on the heels of my refusal. "How much?" He grins again, and I see he is missing a tooth, sporting some hockey-player chic.

"How much you like to spend?" he says, reaching into his pocket.

"Give me two dimes." I pull out a soiled twenty.

"Bien sur," he says, and reaches his hand beneath the table, where I meet it with mine and take one of the bags. He raises an eyebrow at me.

"I just want one," I say. "The other is for her." I point to the spastic girl on the dance floor, who has her hands clamped over her ears and is jumping up and down in place. He looks at her and laughs.

"Really," I tell him, and get up, leaving the twenty on the table. He says something, but I'm turning away, toward the door, and he doesn't follow me. I don't look back to see if he delivers the drugs.

I feel like a white fucking knight as I break out back onto the street. I'll be honest, I used to have a problem. Whenever I'd leave a room, I'd feel like everyone spent the next five minutes talking about me. As if I was the comic relief in all their lives, inserted once every half-hour segment to make them feel good about themselves. I used to worry about that, but not anymore. As long as they're being civil to my face, I can't be fucked about what they really think. And walking out of that bar, back onto the roller coaster of the sidewalk, I know that if they're talking, they're saying some damn good things.

I go to the depanneur on the corner and buy a pack of cigarettes, then hollow one out and fill it with the hash. I smoke it in a doorway, sheltered from the cold, and no one even looks twice as they pass by. It's not very good stuff, but it does the trick, and after I finish it I smoke another, proper cigarette. Once that's finished I feel very good, a little horny and a little buzzed and ready for more action. The street is pulsing before me. My watch says nine, more than an hour late for meeting Ma. But once you're late, you can only get later, so I go looking for a lap dance.

All the clubs have the signs — *danse contacte ici! Frottez vos rêves!* — but only a few really have it, the kind where you can touch everywhere but between the legs. They tell you that before they start, but in a nice enough way that you aren't angry. After a few seconds, you don't even care. They're so magnificent, such warm brown honey all around you. Most of the time, you forget you can touch at all; sometimes I even close my eyes. They say it's for perverts, but it isn't the rubbing or the stroking or the skin

MA BELLE

105

that gets you off. It's that for the length of one song, just a few minutes, a woman makes you think she cares about you more than anything else in the world.

You have to tip at these places. A few dollars for the bouncer who brings me up the stairs. A toonie for the slow-looking girl who takes my coat; she must be the owner's daughter. The other bouncer inside — you tip him before you even shake hands, so he can decide where you're sitting. For a ten I am right against the stage, with a whiskey in my hand before I can sit down.

"How much, doll?" I ask the redhead who brings it to me. Another admission: my sex life is perhaps not as healthy as my looks should allow. Formerly a garden hose of excitement, my cock is now more like a sprinkler: it rises once a day when no one is around, sputters weakly for a few minutes, then beats a guilty retreat back to the cavity it calls home.

"*Dix*," she says.

"Ten fucking dollars?" My twenty is already out, though, flattened on her tray.

She laughs and squeezes my shoulder before heading back to the bar, and I don't bother making a big deal about change. The tip is for her chest and her troubles, and besides, who can be angry in a place like this?

I turn my attention to the pole, shined up and ready for action. The girls love the pole, everyone wants to be the pole. They charm it, seduce it, fuck it. The guy who designed this pole is right up there with the guy who designed the VCR. My two favourite men, the Da Vincis of lust and laziness. So I sit back and watch the pole, waiting to fall in love. Girls walk by in the meantime, dressed in nurses' uniforms, cop outfits and often just lingerie, every outfit the sex store has in stock. It's like some kind of perverse elementary-school Halloween.

I don't ask any of them for a dance. I'm patient. My dream woman has two required qualities — flesh and intensity. Flesh is first. I like them big, but not because that's what turns me on. Most girls can turn me on. Most girls do turn me on. The bigger ones, though, are far more appreciative. I mean, sure, I like the Amazons, but so does every leering drunk in the club. The fat girls, though. They're happy for your interest, grateful for your smiles, and this tends to raise the heat when you take one to the back.

Which is my second thing: I like a girl who's into it, who loves her living. It's not too much to ask someone to enjoy their work. I manage the station, keep the pump boys in tow, I like that just fine. You'll never see me without a fucking smile on, and I don't get paid half of what these girls do. The good ones, at least.

Songs are a good sign of a girl's commitment to the cause, because they pick their own. A broad can easily tune out the latest dance hall butt shaker. I know the glassy look they get in their eyes when they're not really into it. Girls who pick something original, though, for them it's a kick, an indulgence, and they're my favourite. Big girls with bigger tunes and bigger dreams.

I wait through a few tracks, switch my drinks as they switch the girls — four blondes, four whiskeys, forty bucks. When my sweetheart comes on, I know it right away. Her song is some slow rock ballad, the kind that has a bass guitar solo. I love it. I love the girl too, bouncing up on stage. She's not fat, but she's certainly not thin — let's say she overflows in the right places. A black teddy hangs off her like icing on a four-tiered wedding cake. Then it falls, leaving her in a thong that resembles the string around your Sunday roast.

For three minutes I am mesmerized, and she knows it. Her whole body is into the show, even her eyes dance around without their clothes. Her teddy is only a few feet away, so I lean over onto the stage and pull it off to wrap around my drink. I am in lust, the smart man's love. As the song ends, she crawls over to me to pull back the tiny satin shift.

"You do *danse contacte?*" I ask. She does, of course, but I'm polite, right.

"Oui, but I have two more song to dance, monsieur." Her voice rolls off the edge of the stage like a cannonball and hits me in the chest, loaded with seduction.

"A hundred for it now?" I counter. I could wait a few minutes and pay her ten, a good idea given the amount I've already spent on drinks. But I can't even imagine the show she'll put on for a hundred bucks. She smiles, tries not to look too eager. But she wants it, wants me.

"I will talk to the boss," she says. "Maybe just one time." She taps my nose with a single soft brown digit.

Three minutes later we are enclosed in a booth, and her body is everywhere. I can't keep my hands still, I want to touch as much of her as possible. The chairs are sliding to get in my way, and somewhere between my seat and the stall I stumble onto the floor, spilling that fifth whiskey. It had begun to taste rusty anyway. She helps me up, whispers in my ear how handsome I am. Closing the door, she sits in my lap, her ass in my hands, and begins to dance oh slow perfectly slowly. She pushes my head down against her thighs, washing my face with her behind, then straddles me and starts touching herself, so close I only need to stick my tongue out. Finally she returns to my lap, her breasts in my face and her lips on my forehead, brushing back and forth and murmuring something I can't hear but love the sound of. I could do this forever.

When I was eleven, my mother left my dad and me. Just wasn't there one day when we woke up. Took her things in the middle of the night and left. When I asked where she'd gone, he said a vacation, but he took the week off work and spent it sitting on the porch, staring down the road, waiting, hoping for her to come home. The house grew filthy and I ordered myself takeout, scared to shift him from his position on the stoop. And then, one night, she came back. I remember being in bed and seeing the headlights of her car turning into the driveway. The elation I felt at that moment, knowing she was ours again, that's the kind of joy I'm feeling now.

The girl takes a breather as the track switches outside our booth. Even the best of them can't do it without *some* music.

"What is your name?" she says. Her accent is the coquettish French-Canadian they all have, the kind acquired through three years of English in high school and a large number of American clients afterwards. She will most likely die without ever using a contraction.

I tell her and she giggles.

"I am Belle," she says. Bullshit, but it fits. Beauty, it means. Beautiful. She has it, too, she is the perfect kind of beautiful for Montreal. Dark, dirty and burning, an angel with lace-patterned wings.

Suddenly, likely because I'm a fucking stoned drunk idiot, I start to cry. I haven't cried in years, but I put my head against her breast and let it flow, a real grown-up sob fest. She strokes my hair with one hand, then stands up and waves her hands above the booth. She is signalling for us to go, I think. We're leaving together, heading somewhere where we can be properly alone.

"Yes," I say. "Come home with me. That's best, you're right." I gush the words into her chest, maybe run my tongue over her stomach. I pull at her shoulders, try to bring her face toward mine.

Then the door opens with a slam, and there are hands claw-ing at me, pulling me away. I look at Belle as they lift me by my shoulders. She stands, naked and alone, in the doorway of our stall, both hands tight against her mouth, her arms folded over her breasts. Lifting one palm in a wave, she mouths an apology.

MY FEET ARE off the ground and I am being carried, quickly, down through the dark. They throw me out the back door, into the same alley where the dogs had been fighting. A black smear of blood runs several feet along the brick of one wall, perhaps from earlier, although it's slightly above dog height. I dust myself off and throw up against the door. After a moment, I do it again.

Clearing my stomach makes me feel lucid, and staring into my vomit I gain some twisted clarity. I take the remaining hash from my pocket and throw it onto the ground. I don't want it. I don't want drugs, or booze, or sex that comes with a receipt. I want a real job, not the gas station. I'll wear a wool suit with an overcoat and rubber covers for my boots. Use the metro for com-muting, fire people when I have bad days. Kids too; I want an suv full of kids who think their old man isn't so bad. My wife — that'll be Belle. She'll hold me to her chest when I come home, and stroke my hair, and we'll make love as many times as I ask her to. She'll never have headaches. She'll forget her old life to come live with me, and we'll raise our perfect kids in a perfect future, far away from the city and its shiny, seductive cling. With Belle I will sleep soundly every night, the sleep of children in their parents' arms as they are carried from car to bedroom after a long drive home. With Belle I will find peace.

I march around the corner, head high, back toward the strip club entrance. I'm that white knight again, ready to rescue my princess from the tower.

My timing could not be more perfect. At the door, a girl wrapped in a heavy fur coat is leaving. The bouncers walk with her from the club to the cab, and from the way she moves I can tell it's Belle, finished for the night and heading home. I call out, run toward her, but someone moves between us. He reaches from the car and takes her arm, brings her face to his.

My vision is blurry as I race toward them. I keep slipping, but don't fall, just skid forward through the slush. I'm yelling, or someone is, and even though it's cold out, even though my breath is billowing up in big clouds before me, I'm burning with anger. I'm not a big man by any means, but I know how to fight — you go with your forehead, and you go hard.

The bastard shoves Belle into the car when he sees me coming and braces himself against the cab. I barrel into his stomach with both fists, and we go down beside the sidewalk into the filth of the street. Its icy weight pounds the small of my back and I hear him above me, somewhere, yelling for the bouncers. I whip my head forward, hoping to just make contact, but it's too late. I simply accelerate my meeting with his fist. My head shuts off.

When I come to I am being picked up, dragged against a wall. Belle's man swears at me in French, but with the tone of someone teaching his kid brother a lesson. I open my eyes just as the cab door closes, and in that instant I see that the woman isn't Belle at all, just some girl, looking at me in horror, like she can't believe the kind of person I am exists. I close my eyes again and can hear the crowds moving by, stepping over me, unnoticing. I am so lonely in the slush. That's the thing about care: You feel the lack far more than you feel the absence.

IT'S NEARLY MIDNIGHT when I arrive at my mother's, the last of my money spent on a forgiving cab. My eye is swollen shut;

I am a prizefighter without winnings. The snow is freshly fallen in this quieter part of the city, the ground a perfect blanket of white. I use it to wash my face, watching the blood rinse away in my wet palms.

The light in her walk-up is off, but I can see the flashing glow of the television every few seconds. She has so many happy families in that tiny box. My hair is matted against my neck, now fallen completely from its perch. I don't care, though. I surrender. She comes to the door right away when I knock. The look of anger on her face, one I'm sure she's spent hours fuelling, vanishes at the sight of me — wet and bloody and broken.

"Oh, *mon petit*," she moans. "What have they done to you?"

SUCH SIGHTS TO SHOW YOU

MORDECAI JONES met his real father only once, at a bar in Vancouver for lunch. They had mainly middle-aged drunks and confused old men for company, since those are the types who frequent bars at noon. Stan Rogers played on the radio. Mordecai's father wore what had obviously once been a very fine suit, chocolate with tan piping, but it was wrinkled from having been slept in, and there was raspberry jam all down one sleeve. He ordered a BLT with no tomato and a whiskey.

The meal was brief and awkward, and the two men smiled timidly when their forced conversation happened to reveal some common affair between them. They discovered that they had both, in the past, been arrested for similar crimes. But Mordecai had never been to jail. When the bill came, Mordecai's father excused himself to the washroom. He left his wallet, a plastic billfold with a Velcro closure, on the table. His son browsed through it, sliding out enough damp bills to cover his father's share. The pockets of the wallet were filled with pictures of leggy Asian women, but it was obvious they had been torn from magazines and massage-parlour flyers.

"Let's take a walk," his father suggested when they finished. "Looking at the ocean helps settle the stomach, in my experience."

The sun hung fat in the sky, but it was not warm outside. Mordecai put on his jacket and they walked together in silence. After a while, his father reached out and held Mordecai's hand. Passersby stared, but touching his father felt comfortable in a way Mordecai felt uncomfortable describing. The boardwalk was littered with buskers and hustlers, games of three-card monte and a man dancing with a monkey. But the pair stopped for none of them, and ignored most.

At the end of the strip, however, they came upon one show grander than the rest. A boy had submerged himself in a tank of seawater, his torso bound with an armoury of chains and padlocks. Father and son were drawn in by the spectacle like teenagers to the back room of a video store. The escape artist soon broke loose and bobbed freely in the water. Mordecai clapped three times and placed a dollar in a hat at the base of the tank.

His father threw back his head and laughed, startling several other onlookers. The boy, spotting a mark, beseeched the old man to renew the bonds with his own hands. Mordecai's father wordlessly accepted, despite his son's objections, and busily set about securing his diminutive prisoner. After several minutes he gave a satisfied grunt and released the boy into the tank, then went to stand beside Mordecai.

"I've played this game before," he said smugly.

After a minute, the child was still struggling. His efforts to free himself became frantic, and he began to smash his head against the glass walls of the tank. Hysteria and water spilled from the chamber. A woman began to scream. Mordecai, aghast, shouted for help, and turned to see his father calmly yet hastily walking away. Only after moving to stop him did he realize how nothing he could say would turn the man around.

GOING THROUGH CUSTOMS

THE LINEUP AT the Peace Arch crossing was longer than Larry had expected, but not so long that it would be a hassle. There were two lanes open, the right one a few minivans busier. He pulled toward the left, then swerved back at the last second.

"Always a reason the short line's shorter," he said. The rain was beginning to ease up, but the sky seemed to promise another bout any minute. Larry flipped the wipers down a setting. The kid was fidgeting beside him, bouncing his knee and scratching at the beginnings of a beard.

"Try and relax," Larry said. "Measure your breaths or something."

"I'm nervous," Tom said. His face was still boyish, and the depth of his voice kept catching Larry by surprise.

"I'm nervous too," Larry said. "But the shakes aren't going to help either of us, alright? Just take it easy."

"Right," the kid said. "Sorry, I'll get my shit together." He leaned back against the leather of the seat and closed his eyes. "Thanks," he said. "Really ... thanks."

Larry eased off the brake and coasted forward a spot. The steering wheel was damp under his grip. He was nervous too, but he wasn't having any second thoughts.

—

LARRY HAD LEFT Seattle early with hopes of beating the traffic. He figured if he didn't stop for lunch he could easily make it back to Whistler in time for dinner. But the rain was especially bad before sunrise, and the effort required by careful driving quickly wore him out. At around nine he stopped for breakfast and to splash some water on his face. He pulled into a Shell station after eating to fill up before he got back on the highway.

He was leaning against the car watching the meter rise when a kid came out of the station, swinging a thermos in his right hand. The kid's hair was wet, pressed in dark curls against his forehead, and he had a grey wool sweater on over a pair of baggy black jeans. He looked like the kind who spent his lunchtimes in the art room, a real emotional type. Larry pegged him at around eighteen. The kid saw Larry looking and waved. Larry squinted back at him. In his experience, kids didn't have a lot of heart to them anymore, and certainly not the kind of friendliness it took to wave at strangers. Larry raised a hand to his hip and gave a half-hearted wave back. The kid smiled and walked over.

"Nice car," the kid said. Larry had bought himself a Jaguar for Christmas. He had been driving the same Accord for six years, and decided he owed himself an upgrade. It wasn't a flashy Jaguar. Some of his co-workers drove real pin-up cars now, Porsches and Corvettes. Andrew Harris, one of the vice-presidents, even had a Maserati. But Larry didn't like that kind of attention, what his wife Marcie called Viagra on wheels. He just wanted a luxury automobile, plain and simple. In black. So he got one.

"Thanks," he said.

"Canada, huh?" The kid pointed a foot toward Larry's licence plate.

"Yup, just heading home," Larry said. The pump clicked in his hand and he glanced at the meter. He squeezed the pump again, then once more to bring it to an even number.

"Can I come?" the kid said.

Larry laughed.

"No," the kid said, "seriously."

Larry replaced the pump and looked the kid over properly. Closer up, he could see he'd been wrong about the age. Probably nearer to fifteen. His face was pale and smooth, with chubby cheeks and tiny, pouting lips. Good-looking in a cherubic sort of way. Sandals poked out from underneath the jeans, and his toes were red and white from tramping through puddles. The sweater was real wool, the kind grandmothers knit while watching day-time television. The kid had pulled the sleeves down over his hands. The end of the thermos stuck out like a bionic arm.

"Are you kidding?" Larry tore the receipt off the meter and stuffed it in his pocket.

"Nope," the kid said. "I'm on the run."

Larry laughed again. Only in these little highway towns did you get weird shit like this, he thought. If you spent enough time on the road you saw it all. There was a place near Edmonton where you could get free gas if you beat the owner in a fistfight. And another one in Manitoba, just off the Trans-Canada, where all the attendants sang show tunes while they worked.

"It's not funny," the kid said. "I've already come all the way up from Portland."

"From Portland," Larry said. "With a thermos? Don't bullshit me."

"My bag's over there," the kid said. He pointed to a red back-pack leaning against the gas station wall. A pair of muddy sneakers was tied to the front pocket.

Larry sighed. "I'm going to Canada," he said, opening the car door. "California's south. That's where runaways go these days. You're headed in the wrong direction. There's nothing for you in Canada, pal." Larry had a rule about picking up hitchhikers: Don't do it. Marcie would pull over for every guy with dreadlocks and a magic-marker sign if he let her, but it was just a risk you didn't need to take.

"I know that," the kid said, in the defensive tone of the self-righteous adolescent. "I'm not stupid, man. Canada's where I'm going."

"What's your name?" Larry said.

"Tom," the kid said. "Tom Beach."

"Well, Tom," Larry said, "I can't help you. You want ten bucks for a bus, fine. But there's a border between here and Vancouver, and you don't just smile and sign your name on the way by." He pulled his wallet out of his jacket and leafed through a mix of green American and multicoloured Canadian bills. The purple tens stood out like peacocks on a chicken farm. "Here," Larry said, ripping one out and offering it up.

"I don't want money," the kid said. "I want to go to Canada. You can tell them you're my dad at the border. You've got a Jag, man. They're not gonna check you, you know that. I'll bet they just wave you through. Come on."

Larry paused. He had to concede that one to the kid. They could probably get away with it. The border held up visible minorities and unshaven old men in panelled vans, not balding white guys in British sports cars.

"Sorry," Larry said. "But it's not going to happen. Good luck."

He got in the car and closed the door, keeping his head down so he didn't have to see the kid's face.

Tom banged on the window with his fist.

Larry cracked the window. Enough was enough.

"What?" he said.

"Please," the kid said. "I can't go back. It's my stepfather. I'm not fucking with you, please. It's hard to explain, but I can't stay here, you gotta believe me. We're only half an hour away, and you can drop me anywhere as soon as we're over. Please."

Larry stared out toward the highway. The kid sounded afraid. The rain was getting worse, thickening from curtains into walls.

"Get your bag," Larry said. Tom smiled, and Larry knew it was because he thought he understood.

—

LARRY'S PARENTS had split up when he was eleven, and Eric moved in a month later. He and Larry's mother were never married, but once he showed up he never left. Larry liked him at first. He came to Larry's football games, which Larry's father had never done, and knew things men were supposed to know, like how to change the oil and open a beer bottle with your teeth. Best of all, he looked like Dave Kingman, then centre fielder for the Chicago Cubs. That year, 1979, Kingman hit forty-eight homers and drove in a hundred and fifteen runs. Larry knew everything there was to know about Dave Kingman. Born in Pedleton, Oregon. Attended the University of Southern California. Interests included movies and history. Eric had Kingman's hard jaw and close-set eyes, creating such a resemblance that he was often stopped for autographs. With a wink in Larry's direction, he always signed with a flourish.

Larry's mother worked an hour away, in the cosmetics department at the Marshall Field's downtown. She had to take the first train into the city every weekday, which meant she was always in bed by ten.

Eric would come into Larry's room after she was asleep. He would stand beside the bed for a long time before getting in, listening to the boy breathe. Larry fought back the first few times, but Eric was a heavy man, and Larry soon learned that if he didn't struggle he wouldn't get hit.

Most of those memories faded as he grew older, eroded by a combination of denial and time. But some things could not be forgotten. The way the bed would sink and groan under Eric's weight. The names he would whisper in Larry's ear. *Baby, pretty boy, Prince Charming.* And his hands. He had hands like a hobgoblin. Thick knuckles and rough palms, fingernails that cut when they squeezed. Sometimes, when Larry woke up sweating and cotton-mouthed in the middle of the night, he could still feel those hands clawing at his hips.

Once, when Eric had finished, Larry asked him when it would end, when Eric would have everything he wanted. He only snickered, his breath warm and rancid against the back of Larry's neck, and murmured that it never had to. Two weeks later Larry left school after lunch and boarded a bus to Detroit. By the end of the year he was living out of a hostel in Calgary, cleaning hotel rooms during the day and bussing tables at night. He was fifteen.

———

"READY?" Larry said. Aside from discussing the particulars of their deception, the two had exchanged only a few words on the ride up. The kid, Larry realized gladly, seemed to understand that their partnership was a temporary one.

"Yeah. We'll be fine," Tom said. "I've got a good feeling about this." Larry wondered at the kid's newfound confidence, but decided it was admirable. When Larry had come to Canada it had been easier, just a hop off the bus and a run through the bushes and the imaginary line was crossed. But that was before people had so many things to be afraid of.

The line moved turtle steady, and within a half hour they pulled into a pending position so the camera could snap the plates. The car before them, a blue station wagon, had trouble. The driver looked relaxed, her arm flopped casually out the window. But the guard kept asking questions.

After a few minutes he got out of his booth and walked around the car, then knocked on the back. The driver got out. She was short, mid-forties, with black, frizzy hair and a purple dress that bunched at her hips and ended too soon, several inches above her knees. She moved quickly, but Larry could see the sudden effort to her casualness, as if she were a shoplifter and candy bars were beginning to tumble out from beneath her shirt. Under the guard's watch, she opened the trunk. It was empty, aside from a pink blanket and some untaped hockey sticks. The guard said something to her, made a brief, dismissing hand gesture, and walked back to his booth. By the time he sat down the Volvo was gone, plowing ahead toward the freedom of the Great White North.

Larry and the kid drove forward.

"Citizenships." The guard was Asian, not much more than twenty, with a wide brow and prominent cheekbones beneath his shaved head. Larry felt he looked well suited to authority, the kind of guy who would be just as comfortable in a firehouse or police station.

"We're both Canadian," Larry said.

"Where do you live?"

"In Whistler."

The guard glanced up from his computer.

"Still some good days up there, or is the season finished?" he asked.

"No, it's still pretty good," Larry said. "I actually got out for a little last weekend." He wanted to look over at the kid and see how he was holding up, but he couldn't.

"Good, good to hear," the guard said. "What were you doing down in the States?"

"Just went down to see the Science Centre, checked out that new exhibit there." This detail was the key to their lie, gleaned from a brochure Larry had browsed through that morning while checking out of the hotel.

The guard seemed to notice Tom for the first time, and leaned forward slightly to peer into the car.

"This your son?" he said.

"Yes," Larry said, with what he worried was too much eagerness. Easy, he thought, the hard part is almost over. Easy does it.

"No school today, buddy?" the guard said.

"No, none this week," Tom said with a thumbs-up. "It's spring break."

Larry winced and held his breath. The thumb was overboard, even if the kid did it with surprising sincerity. His cheeks were getting flushed.

The guard nodded slowly.

"Spring break already, huh?" he said. "I thought spring break wasn't for a couple of weeks yet. Haven't seen the MTV specials or anything." Larry held his breath.

"It is," Tom said. "I mean, you're right. It isn't for a couple of weeks. For other kids, I mean." The guard cocked an eyebrow, and Larry turned to look at Tom. The kid's eyes were wild, his brain working furiously behind them. He was losing his grip.

"He's home-schooled," Larry said. "So I gave it to him early."

The guard nodded again, but slower this time.

"You want to open up the trunk for me, sir?" he said.

"Sure, of course." Larry turned the car off and hit the trunk release on his keychain. There was a pop as it unlocked, and the guard stepped down from the booth. Larry watched him through the side mirror, walking slowly around to the back of the car. His boots crunched on the pavement.

"You got anything in there?" Tom said.

"No," Larry said. "Don't look back, we're fine. Just don't say anything."

The guard came back around, carrying something.

"What is this?" He stuck his hand through the driver-side window, inches from Larry's face. It held a thick roll of silver duct tape. Larry laughed.

"Duct tape?" he said.

"Yeah, I'm aware of that," the guard said. "Why do you have so much of it? I'd say there's a dozen rolls back there." He pulled the tape back and leaned down to the window. His face was very close, Larry could see the stains on his teeth. Larry laughed again.

"Yeah, I've been doing renos on our house. Winter left some holes in the roof, you know. Duct tape fixes anything. I guess I just didn't bother unloading it for the drive down." The guard sighed, then stood up and cradled the duct tape in his hands. For almost a minute, no one said anything. He walked back to the trunk again, then closed it with a thump.

"Go ahead," he shouted, and the Jaguar rolled forward.

The kid waited ten seconds or so, then turned in his seat to see out the back window. He pumped his fist.

"Alright!" he said. "He didn't even ask us if we had anything to declare, man!"

"That's Canada for you," Larry said.

"Holy shit. Holy shit!" Tom was bouncing.

Larry smiled. Until this moment, he realized, the kid had probably seen Canada as more geography than nation, just a giant red space on the map. The rain misted as the sun cautiously began to peek through the clouds. Larry took the first exit, into White Rock. He pulled over into a parking lot by the side of a park and opened the car door, stretching his legs and yawning.

Tom hopped out and just stood by his door, staring around at a place that was entirely new, yet exactly like the one he just left. Larry walked around the front of the car.

"Okay?" he said.

"Yeah, more than okay," the kid said.

"You need money or anything? If you know where you're going, I can take you. I mean, I drive right through the city to get to Whistler." Larry pulled out his wallet, fingering three twenties.

"No, it's fine," Tom said. "I'm pretty good at this kind of stuff, I'll figure something out. Just, you know, thanks. You saved my life, man. Really."

"Yeah, no, I was happy to help," Larry said. He pushed the twenties at the kid, who hesitated a second before grabbing them and balling them into his pocket.

"Really, you don't have to," the kid said.

"Good luck." Larry stuck out his hand.

"Thanks. Thanks. I won't forget you, man." They shook quickly, Larry's hand pumping the kid's weak wrist, and Tom jogged away toward a bus station at the edge of the parking lot.

Peace Arch Park had been built to celebrate the creation of the border crossing. It was mostly just a big lawn, but thirty feet from Larry a father was pushing his son and daughter on a swing set. He had to race back and forth from swing to swing to keep them both going. He was laughing between gasps for air, and his children screamed and laughed with him.

The father saw Larry watching and stopped pushing, then walked around the front of the swings. Larry raised his hand, but then realized the sun was behind him and thus the father could see only his silhouette. Then the kids yelled, their swings were slowing and they needed a push, and their father turned back to them.

Larry turned too, back to the Jaguar and the drive home to Whistler. The sun was out properly now, and he wanted to get going before afternoon traffic hit. He turned on a talk radio station and began to look for signs pointing back to the highway.

Then Larry caught the lights in his rear-view mirror. The glare from the sun had concealed them until they were right behind him, red and blue flashes that made his left leg begin to tremble. All his pores filled with sweat. The cruiser came right up behind him, and he pulled slowly off to the right. His mouth tasted like gasoline. It had been a stupid risk to take. Of course the search on his plates would bring up his record, all those secrets he had tried so hard to put behind him. They had told him no warnings, the first offense would be his last.

But the cop didn't stop, swerving around him and shooting to the end of the street before skidding into a right and vanishing. Larry pulled over anyway and brought the Jaguar to a stop. He let himself slump forward, and measured his breaths while the cool leather of the steering wheel pressed against his forehead. They never would have believed him, that this time was different. An apology, an attempt to make all the others right. He had never meant to hurt anyone. The rest of the way home, he would drive very cautiously.

A ROUTINE TO THESE THINGS

THE PIANIST WAS playing frenetically, so fast the notes were running together, and the effort of it was making him sweat. From where I was sitting I could see how his forehead shone with it. He wasn't bald, but his hair seemed to start very far back, like he was looking into a fan. He was smiling while he played, his fingers pounding faster than I could follow. I wondered if the keys were really made of ivory. How many elephants go into a piano? Sounds like half a joke.

I felt Angela shift in the chair beside me. I wanted to turn and see what was making her fidget, but then she would feel me looking, and that would imply things. So instead I looked away — at the pianist, at the stage, at the audience. The men all looked uncomfortable in their tuxedos. It was very hot, I could feel beads growing inside my armpits and escaping down the sides of my chest. I wondered if Angela was shifting because she was hot too. But I didn't look over. Her smell was enough. I felt it creeping up my nostrils and around my brain. Experienced yet youthful, like a sexy first-grade teacher. I had seen the smoked orange bottle on her dresser a thousand times, but I could never remember its name.

We had been separated for almost four months. This evening was the beginning of our reconciliation attempt, a first date that wasn't. It had been the longest four months of my life. Even now, beside her, I felt time slouching forward.

The music grew louder for a moment, swelling up triumphantly before settling back down. I don't know how you increase the volume on a piano. He must have been hitting the keys harder.

LAST WINTER WAS the first time since Liam's birth that we had been able to travel — five seemed old enough to leave him with his grandparents for a week — and we flew down to Florida to get some rest beneath the sun. Angela had a friend, Jessica, who lived there; an old roommate, she had moved to Miami to open an advertising firm. On our last night in town we went to a party at her house, a sprawling art deco goliath in Coconut Grove. A swinger's party. Jessica had invited us the night before, after we had been out to dinner and had several bottles of overpriced shiraz.

I didn't say anything at the hotel when Angela put on her fancy blue bra with white lace around the cups. I should have, in retrospect. By keeping silent, I tacitly agreed to the whole thing. But I wanted her to be the one to reconsider.

"Ready?" she said, as the taxi pulled up to Jessica's house. Even then I just smiled back and nodded, hoping she would interpret something from my silence. Perhaps it made sense that we were doing this. Since Liam had been born, our sex life had become predictable and pathetic. But there must have been a better way than messing around with strangers.

There's a routine to these things, a little ritual they do so that no one gets left out. I didn't imagine it like that. I don't know how I had imagined it, but not like that. I guess I thought it would be more like trading hockey cards at recess. My wife plus a Bobby Orr for your wife and two Tony Espositos. But it was even more impersonal.

All the men wrote their names on cards when they came in, and all the cards went in a bowl, a little glass trinket with a painted dolphin on its bottom. Then everyone had a good time, slowly getting drunk enough to forget their nerves while checking each other out.

I found myself double-shifted, trying to prevent other men from staring at Angela while keeping an eye on all their wives. The party was loaded with Miami Beach players, sleazy guys in pastel button downs and their bottle-blonde partners. Angela looked good; she had on a pale blue cocktail dress she'd bought at Bloomingdale's on the day we arrived. That and a pair of silver sandals with raised heels.

She kept by my side for the beginning of the evening. I held her hand as much as possible, and she seemed to appreciate that, squeezing my fingers as we made polite conversation with the other couples. After an hour or so she went to the washroom, and I wandered around. Two women, tan and blonde and in their early twenties, were chatting on a couch, and as I passed by they paused to look me up and down. They were attractive enough that I enjoyed it, but it also made me anxious to think that the same appraisals were being conducted on Angela.

I briefly struck up a conversation with a guy who looked like the arch-villain in an action movie. He couldn't have been more than forty, but his hair was totally white, devoid of any colour whatsoever. An ivory linen suit hung over his broad frame, and he had his shirt unbuttoned to the middle of his chest. He was German, also in town visiting.

"This is your first time? You have never been to one of these before?" he said.

"Can you tell?"

"A little." He shrugged. "To be honest, you don't look like you're enjoying yourself. You need to relax. There are some beautiful women here."

"Yeah, no," I said. "It's just ... you know, first time, like you said. Virgin nerves."

"You're lucky." He squeezed his thumb and forefinger together. "Triple-A grade here. A very good crop for your first time, boss."

I didn't answer and we stood without saying anything for a moment. He kept looking over my shoulder, even though his wife, an Amazon, was standing behind him. After a few minutes I grew frustrated with his crowd-scanning and excused myself. I found Angela at the back of the house, by the pool. She was talking to two men in jeans and dark dress shirts. One had long hair, Samsonian curls down to his shoulders, and the other was bald. This was, to my eye, all that differentiated them. They sized me up as I approached, and I put my hand on Angela's shoulder from behind. She turned around. Her face was flushed.

"Are you having fun?" she asked. But before I could answer Jessica's voice floated toward us, calling everyone inside.

"I don't want to do this," I said to Angela as we walked in. If she heard, she pretended not to. I tried to pull her back by her hand but we were already in the living room, with a crowd pressing behind us, and leaving would have meant making a scene.

Jessica moved to the centre of the room with the bowl in hand. She wore a slinky black dress that ended just below her ass, revealing two toned brown thighs. Her husband, Vaughn, who hadn't come to dinner the previous night, but whom I'd met earlier that evening, was a record producer. He was sprawled over a club chair in the corner of the room, wearing sunglasses and flicking a lighter on and off, staring at the flame.

"Ladies, are you ready to meet your evening's entertainment?" Jessica said. There were some hoots from within the crowd — I'd guess we totalled about a dozen couples — and Angela tore her hand away from mine to clap. My mouth felt dry.

"Angela, you're up first!" Jessica said, casting a look in my direction that I couldn't really interpret. I imagine she saw me as an interloper, someone who had taken her college friend and settled her down, burdening her with a child too early. Jessica had several kids, but all had been inherited from Vaughn's previous marriage.

Without looking back at me, Angela waded through the crowd and stood, expectant, before the bowl.

"Cover your eyes!" Jessica said. Angela did so with her left hand, and with her right reached into the bowl, grabbing at the first card her fingers touched. Jessica snatched it from her.

"Karl!" she bellowed. The German I'd been talking to stepped forward, patting me on the shoulder as he moved past. It all happened very quickly. He took Angela's hand, and they moved toward the hallway leading to the bedrooms that the women had been pre-assigned. As they reached the hallway, Angela whirled around. Her eyes searched for mine, and, finding them, she mouthed me an "I love you" before disappearing down the corridor. I sank onto an open couch, holding my drink to my forehead and rolling it back and forth above my eyebrows.

Soon after my own name was drawn by a mousy brunette named April. I hadn't met her earlier, but she had no trouble picking me out from the rapidly shrinking cluster of men.

She was wearing a short black skirt and pink blouse, unbuttoned to show a fair share of her pointy, not insignificant breasts. Under normal circumstances I likely would have been attracted to her.

April led me down the hall and around the corner to what must have been Vaughn's daughter's room. His kids were all away, shipped for the night to a Christmas party at their real mother's place, another McMansion in the next community down the highway. The bed had a pink duvet with canary-yellow pillows. Above the bed hung a poster of some teen heartthrob. In the corner of the room was a desk that I recognized as the same kind Angela and I had bought for Liam only a few weeks before, a cheap unit designed to look expensive. It had taken me hours to snap together. Seeing it here made me think of him, and that made me feel sick.

April turned the lights off as we entered, but the moon shone through the window and turned everything blue, giving us nowhere to hide. We undressed facing away from each other, and when I turned around she was still stepping out of her panties. I slid under the covers and she came at me wordlessly, all wet mouth and groping hands. My eyes were heavy from the cocktails.

There was a knocking sound coming from the wall — a headboard in the adjacent room. April tugged sharply at my cock. Her hands were smaller than Angela's. Without warning she paused, then suddenly pulled away. I felt embarrassed at remaining erect, even though she couldn't see me in the dark. We were silent for a few moments.

"You all right?" I eventually said. I was unsure of the etiquette for the situation.

"I'm sorry," April said. I could hear the tears in her throat. "It's ... I'm really sorry. I've never done this before." I wish I could have seen her face. "I'm just worried about my husband."

"Oh," I said. "That's fine." I felt disgusting and guilty, like some greasy lothario. "Listen, that's fine. How about we just lie down?

You want me to ... what do you want?" I could still hear the knocking against the wall while I waited for her to answer. Underneath it, a woman's muffled moan was beginning to leak through. I strained to identify the voice, then decided I didn't want to know.

"Can we?" April said. "I'm sorry. Yeah, let's just lie down." Her voice was steadying a little. I grabbed my pants from the floor and pulled them on beneath the covers, then lay straight, facing the ceiling. I felt her weight settle beside me and reached out an arm toward her. She stiffened at my touch, and I withdrew to one side of the bed.

"Thanks," she said. "Really. I was so worried this would happen." I couldn't avoid listening to the moaning; it was growing louder. Angela's were short and high. I'd lived with my older brother in a tiny walk-up when the two of us first began dating, and she used to hold a pillow against her mouth to stifle them.

"Hey, no problem," I said, and I could sense the distraction in my own voice. "We'll just hang out until we hear some other people in the hall, right?" I didn't want to wait. I wanted to start knocking on doors until we found our spouses. I understood how each couple would try and avoid being the first back into the living room, since the group gathering after sex would inevitably be more awkward than the one preceding it. But I didn't care. I imagined myself stalking up and down the hallway, barging in on couple after couple until I found Angela, her ass in the air while Karl pounded at her like a woodpecker. How she would look up at me, standing clothed and afraid in the doorway, and be disappointed. Disappointed that I hadn't gone through with it. Disappointed that I had made us the gossip of the party, the conservative Canadian couple who got scared off by a little swapping. And disappointed that I'd shown up before Karl could finish her off.

I rolled over in the bed and tried to send my mind away.

There was a clock with glowing hands on the nightstand, and I watched them count out an hour, one slow glowing streak and one fast one, chasing each other around and around and around. The moans continued for forty-two minutes.

ANGELA WOKE ME as the sun was rising, shaking me from where I'd eventually fallen asleep by the pool, my suit jacket bunched beneath my head. I stared woozily up at her from the concrete. I had plotted my first line a dozen times before falling asleep, but nothing sounded right.

"Good night?" I said.

"What?"

"Did you have fun, last night?"

She pursed her lips and looked away, then went to find Jessica to say goodbye.

Although we never stated it explicitly, there was some agreement never to discuss that evening. I think she understood that I was afraid of what she might say. On the cab ride back to the hotel, we stared out opposite windows. I watched the empty beach roll past, and beyond it the ocean.

From that point on we couldn't quite become comfortable again, in or out of the bedroom. I'd snap at her for tiny things — forgetting groceries, leaving papers around the house, Liam. Our conversations seemed to veer toward monosyllables, and before long we were only speaking when it was necessary. My trust was just gone. It had never been an issue before, but now I found myself needing to know where she was every minute of the day. I'd call her phone at random times, then panic if she didn't answer. I varied my work schedule in attempts to catch her at home with someone else. I checked her e-mail with military regularity. Not once did I find anything to heighten my suspicions. But I could not dampen them either.

It came to a head one evening after we'd been out for dinner. The food had been great, the wine unparalleled. Yet it had been like eating a meal at a retirement home. Other than discussing the menu, I don't think we exchanged more than a dozen sentences. On the drive home I played the radio while she slept. As we pulled into the driveway, she woke up and, in a voice barely above a whisper, she asked me if I still loved her. She was staring straight ahead, into the pooled light from the garage door. I think I laughed.

"Angela," I said. I let us sit in silence for a few heartbeats, because I didn't want my answer to seem rushed. "Of course I still love you." My hand reached across toward her knee, but her legs were gathered near the door. "Are you being serious?"

"Yes." Her eyes were downcast as she ran a nail along the seam of her pants. She left the word hanging, like she meant to follow it with a thought but instead decided to go with just one word.

"Do you still love me?" I felt the tone of my voice change from joking to sombre.

"I don't know." My stomach clenched. "Babe, I don't know if I do." The car's trip odometer read four hundred and eleven miles. "I mean, Simon, I still love you, of course. Just lately … lately you're not the person I fell in love with. Does that make any sense?" I wondered when it had been reset, or if it had just maxed out and started over. "And I don't know what's happened to you, or to us, but I can't handle this anymore. I mean, I'm not happy." Had I been trying to measure something with it? The drive to work? "I think we maybe need a change. A serious change."

I nodded, reset the odometer with a punch, and got out of the car. I went to bed immediately, and she didn't join me until much later. She stroked my hair as I pretended to sleep, and whispered, crying now, that she wanted me to make love to her. "Please," she said. I wanted to. I wanted to be amazing and then leave, show her what she had and then pull it away. But I decided it would be better to act hurt, convinced that she would change her mind about everything when she saw me so affected. So I skulked off to sleep on the couch. Within a week, I'd moved out of our house and into an apartment by my office.

I WANTED TO lean over and grab her hand now, but I was worried. We'd kissed at the house, but only briefly, and in front of Liam. I wanted to hold her hand and so I wasn't holding it. I felt like a teenager in a movie theatre, waiting to see if his date would use the armrest or cross her wrists between her legs. Angela's hands were folded, one over the other, in her lap. I took a deep breath and focused on the music. It was all high notes now, a rapid stop-and-start tinkling like Liam's tentative pisses when he was forced to raise himself up to a urinal. Farther down our row I spotted a man engrossed by the music. He had a high collar on, like a priest would wear, but I couldn't see if that was what he was. His fingers danced above his knees like tiny conductors, but he was behind the music by at least a few notes. He kept going, though, right to the end of the piece, always a few bars late.

THEY WERE FILMING a movie at the house — our house — last week, when I went to ask Angela to this concert. When I'd moved out, I had assumed that I'd still be paying all her bills, but after I'd been gone for a month she told me she had rented the house — an old Victorian by the ferry terminal, a real one-of-a-kind, painted all white, sunshine in every corner — to some producer, and that he was paying her several thousand a week to make his movie there. She and Liam were given a complimentary suite at The Empress so they could be out of the house during filming, but the room had given Liam nightmares and Angela decided it would be less hassle to just live around the crew.

"Are you sleeping with this producer?" I'd asked over the phone. I'd thought if I surprised her with the question I would be more likely to get an honest answer.

"Fuck you." She hung up, and I'd had to call back.

"Sorry, I just wanted to know."

"You always want to know, that's the problem." From the way her voice grew softer I imagined she was reaching away from the phone for a moment, into the fridge or a dresser.

"So, does that ... I mean, you're not. Right?"

"Simon, you're ridiculous. Are you coming by for Liam this afternoon? It's been a long day, I really can't deal with this right now."

"Yeah, right, I'm sorry. I'll be by after work."

And what a workday it had been! Every twenty minutes into the bathroom to check on my skin and my hair, making sure I looked presentable. I couldn't ever remember being so concerned about my appearance, so conscious of every pockmark, every thin hair and sagging lump of skin. Still, at the barber on the way over, I felt good. I looked polished, and confident, and these are the things they tell you women find most important. When I had first joined the firm, during the market's headier days, there would be balls and dinners every weekend. Angela had loved standing before me, tucking corners and running her fingers through the back of my hair. I'd been a doll for her to trot out and admire.

I rang the doorbell when I arrived. I'd installed it myself.

The last one had broken suddenly, just after we'd moved in, and Angela and I had awoken one morning to the monotone of the bell, ringing unprovoked. I'd run downstairs, a pillow around my ears, and pushed pleadingly at the button, but to no avail.

Angela came down behind me. She thought it was hilarious, and laughed even harder when I took a hammer from the garage and began swinging at the doorframe, me in my pajama pants and glasses.

She screamed, running out onto the lawn in her nightgown. It was early, the sun was just rising, and the street was covered in fog. I stopped to stare at her fading in and out of it like some Vancouver Island Lady of the Lake.

I took a final swing at the doorframe, and sent the lock, the doorbell mechanism and a shower of wood out onto the front steps. The ringing stopped. Angela ran up the lawn into my bare arms.

"My saviour, my hero," she moaned into my chest. I carried her inside and we made love like that, on the stairs, the front door swinging open onto the morning behind us.

No one was answering the doorbell now. I rang it again. There was a van parked outside. Two minutes, then again. I was growing agitated; what would I do if no one was home? Then I heard the shuffling of Liam's footsteps and he opened the door, his head barely reaching the knob.

"Don't open the door, little man." I stepped inside and gathered him up in my arms. He'd just had a bath and smelled of soap. His nose was running; I wiped it with my sleeve. "You don't know who could be out there."

"Hi, Dad," he buried his head into my shoulder. He was getting heavier, and I sighed from the strain of lifting him. "I thought it was Tom. He said he would be back soon."

"Who's Tom?" I set him down on those stairs. The house was not my house, I noticed for the first time. Every room was different, filled with new furniture, new artwork, new books and new rugs. New, new, new; it was like being at an open house. Even the pictures had different people in them. It was a pretend house for a pretend family.

"Tom is the movie man." He jumped up off the stairs. "He is making our movie. Fantastic." Fantastic was Liam's favourite word. I can't remember when he started using it, but now it seemed to be everywhere.

"Where did he go?" I walked around, peeking into rooms that I thought I'd known. The den was filled with cameras and lighting equipment, cords coiled around them all in a protective, snakelike ring.

"Tom has gone to Site B." Liam held my hand and trailed behind me. I could feel him playing with the hem of my suit jacket with his free hand, idly toying the corner between his fingers.

"Where's that, babe?" The kitchen appliances were all new, our early-nineties models replaced by the brushed steel of an espresso machine and fruit juicer.

"I don't know. Do you want to sing happy birthday, Dad?"

"Why? Whose birthday is it?"

"Nobody's. Mine is in four months and twelve days."

"It is. What would you like for your present, pal?" I had scooped him up again and brought him upstairs. The master bedroom was the only room left in its original state. The bed was unmade; the blankets lay bunched at the end. I wondered if that meant both sides had been slept in. I thought about going to smell it.

"I want a bike. A fantastic one. Also ... Lego. Also ... I really want Lego. And I want Jason to come." Jason Tagliatelli lived down the block. His father Paul was a mob boss. Angela had been worried about their friendship, but I'd encouraged it. In fact, I always went to pick Liam up when he was playing at Jason's. I loved shaking hands with Paul, swapping small talk.

"Jason can come, definitely. We'll bring all your buddies." Liam's room was empty. No, not empty. There were dolls in it, hung from the ceiling. Not girly dolls, but marionettes. They were white, like they'd been bleached. No eyes, no nose, and tiny crimson smiles. There must have been two dozen of them, suspended limp and happy. The room was almost airless, they didn't seem to swing at all. They just were.

"Those are the monsters." Liam had wandered off and then come back. He stood in the doorway, watching me run my hand over one of the figures. It felt like a cutting board.

"The monsters, huh?"

"Yes. Our movie is a hoary movie. Fantastic."

"A horror movie. Where's all the stuff from your room?" I closed the door.

"Basement. I get to sleep with Mum every night now." Case closed on that one.

"Well, you're a lucky fellow. Where's Mum now?" We went back to the kitchen, I'd had my fill of exploring.

"Don't know, don't know. Lisa is here. Want me to get her?" Lisa was Liam's babysitter, a fourteen-year-old on the losing end of what I predicted would be a life-long battle with acne. A nice enough girl, though.

"No, no, that's fine." I should have made it clearer to Angela that I had wanted to see her as well. I rooted around for some paper to leave her a note, but the kitchen was too spotless. No letters on the counter, no bills in the drawers. I used a receipt from my pocket.

*Hi babe — maybe wanted to see if you felt like doing something.
I know we haven't talked about it yet, but it's been almost four months.
I know*

I crumbled that up and fished another receipt from my pocket.

*Hi babe — Extra ticket to piano concerto on Sun. Interested?
Love, S.*

I considered drawing a heart or something, but that seemed ridiculous. Besides, I was worried Tom or some other movie man would be in here first and think I was soft.

I took Liam out for hamburgers and ice cream. He rolled the window down in the car and stuck his hand out, spilling jailbars of light onto the space between us.

"Dad," he said, "why?" Strange that the question came now, after I'd already been gone for so long. I had waited for it a while, then decided it would never come. Now that it had, I was no longer prepared, and pretended not to hear him. He didn't ask again. Angela called me that night, and after some discussion decided she would be happy to come.

THERE WAS AN intermission, and we went out into the lobby to get a drink. She walked before me with a swagger I'd only noticed a few times before. It was the one she used when she wore lingerie, or a low-cut top.

We stood away from the crowd with our drinks, leaning against a railing that overlooked another, lower lobby. I imagined letting my vodka slip away over the edge, watching it fall at instant replay speed, tumbling onto the crowd below. The floor below was carpeted; the glass wouldn't even shatter.

"How's the film coming?" I didn't look at her. I was finding it hard to make eye contact.

"I don't know, to be honest. I'm out mostly during the day,

and when I'm home I try and keep out of their way."

"Isn't it intrusive, their always being around like that?"

"A little. They're good about giving me my space. I really have no control over things. I signed it all away, so there's no point in complaining." She stood up straight, but I remained leaning.

"Is Liam all right with it?"

"Fine."

Another pause. I wanted to be funny, or charming. Normally I never had trouble talking, but this … I wanted to get to issues, resolve things, and I knew that would only upset her. I needed to keep it light, but my tongue was leaden. She put her hand on my back.

"Watched any good TV lately?" Horrible.

"I don't really have the time; I've been trying to get out with Liam more."

"Right." Right. I stood up and faced her. She was growing older. I could see the lines forming at her eyes and the points of her mouth, crevices just beginning to appear. I had wondered, before we were married, about how she would age. I had envisioned, I guess, that she would be the kind of mother Liam's friends would whisper about in secret, possessed of that mature sexuality so few women attain without sacrificing their class. She had done it, I saw now, or was doing it. Her eyes looked over my shoulder, out a long bank of windows across from us. They looked out over the water, onto the harried lights of the city.

"Were there others?" It burst forth like a cough. She didn't answer, but her eyes came back to mine. They were sad, I saw, sad for me. Sympathetic eyes.

"Still? Still?" She looked down and took a long sip from her drink. "There's no answer I can give you that will make you any happier, Simon."

"I know, I'm sorry. It's just ... if there was a letter on the table, and you knew it had bad news inside, would you open it anyway?"

"No, Simon, I wouldn't. I just want to be as happy as I can. I'm having a lovely night. I *was* having a lovely night. Can we get back to that?" The speakers in the lobby came on with a scratch, and a bell tinkled to signal the end of the intermission.

"Of course, babe." I smiled, wide and toothy. "I'm having a lovely night too."

I'D BEEN WITH one other woman during our separation. I had struggled for a while over the decision. Was Angela seeing someone else? Would she be upset if she knew I was? I felt, for the first month, that I was better off staying single, getting focused on work, exercising. Every morning I did a hundred sit-ups against the foot of my bed. It was self-improvement, and it invigorated me, briefly. Finally, I called a telephone dating service.

It was ridiculous, describing myself into the receiver. Played back to me, my voice sounded old and professorial, pathetic. I drank some scotch and tried again. Pretending I'd just heard a joke, I attempted to inject a sprightlier, laughing tone into my voice. It didn't work, and I replaced my little monologue six times before I was fed up, and just left it.

The next day, though, three replies. One from another man, which I allowed to conclude before deleting, my face burning hot in the dark of my adopted bedroom. One from an older woman, almost fifty, who asked quite frankly about my fertility. The last one was a woman in her mid-thirties. Her voice sounded husky, like a phone sex operator's. I wondered if it was as rehearsed as mine. I replied, she replied again, and we set up a dinner at a Mexican place downtown. I felt ashamed about it, but lustfully optimistic. When I left the apartment to meet her, I unplugged the phone in case I brought her home and Angela called.

Sheila. She was gorgeous; the taut lines of her body and the bounce of her hair reminded me of my university days. But she carried herself with a kind of insecurity that made everything else seem the result of effort and affectation. She was beautiful, but at a cost. Also she was too tall, nearly six feet.

Dinner was awkward, a bizarre combination of chit-chat and confession. She had a patch of brown freckles at her throat, and I spent a great deal of time wondering if they continued down to her breasts. She told me about her marriages, two, which had both ended in messy divorces. The result, she admitted, was that she was financially stable but emotionally wasted. I said I was divorced too, but recently.

"Did it hurt, right afterwards?"

"Of course, horribly." Four glasses of Mission Hill in, I was enjoying my lie like a finely cut suit, testing how it felt, how it moved, how it looked from different angles.

"It is horrible, that feeling of loneliness." She looked away from the table and bit her lip. Angela never cried in public. That made her tears when we were alone all the more endearing.

We slept together. I went to her place, an apartment downtown by the water, one of who knows how many units in one of who knows how many buildings.

It was good sex, infused with a barely remembered urgency. It was emancipating, like I was regaining something I had lost, something I hadn't known I needed. When it was over, though, I broke into a nervous sweat. My lust shot, I simply felt scared. Scared by her tanned, foreign body. Her foreign bed, her foreign smell, they forced me out into the night with a hasty, confused kiss to the cheek. She called several times the following week, then gave up.

ANGELA AND I rose with the audience for a standing ovation. The old man came out for an encore, and played two pieces, one fast and one very slow, a funeral march.

I sometimes look at life like that — one great cyclical mess of slow parts and fast parts. The fast parts are the short periods when everything seems to happen all at once — death, divorce, destitution, births, romance, windfalls, happiness. The low points can last for years, a sober string of days filled with nothing more than a commute and a paycheque. It's depressing to think about, this great, undulating line doggedly pacing out one's life, and along it, all these points, tiny moments marking out highs and lows and in-betweens. It sometimes obsesses me, especially when I'm happy, because just when everything seems good, exactly in the place I want, I begin to worry that I'm peaking, and the next day the descent will begin anew, back into the sludge of everyman's reality. That's the problem, of course. You never know when you're at the top.

I smiled at Angela as we stood up again, and she leaned over and gave me a brief kiss on the cheek. I raised my eyebrows at her, and must have smiled. I led the way through the crush of the departing crowd, all funnelling toward the exit. I put my hand out and grabbed her shoulder, pulling her with me through the masses. Then I realized it wasn't her, but another woman entirely. Angela had moved ahead already, she was waiting for me outside, just beyond the doors. In a moment, I would join her.

ANIMALS

THAT ELVIS FESTIVAL was one to remember, because it was then I first met Allison. I don't know why they have that festival at all, since I bet Elvis never once even heard of British Columbia, much less Penticton. Big though, it's a big thing, and I met her there one night after I had lost fifty bucks playing Caribbean stud.

She was in the little parking lot between the casino and the hotel, just standing around like she was waiting for someone, and I walked right up to her. She had on blue jeans and sandals and a white shirt that looked big enough to be her daddy's. She had a good face though, shaped like a heart and pretty, even without makeup.

Who you waiting for, I said.

My boyfriend, she said, but she looked down as she said it because she could probably see from how I was standing that I was thinking about taking her home.

Where is he, I said.

I don't know, she said, smiling, and she didn't seem scared at all. I thought to myself that this was maybe too easy.

Well, I said, how about I'll come back around here in

half-an-hour's time, and if he's not here, you and I'll make up for him. I slipped my arm around her waist as I said it, but she stepped away and laughed.

I don't think so, she said, he wouldn't like that. But I knew then from her laughing that things would be just fine.

So I went back into the casino and sat around at the bar with Geoff, and we had a beer or two together and looked at all the Elvises walking around. Old Elvises, women Elvises, midget Elvises. Geoff said over five hundred Elvises were in town for just that weekend. There were even some Black and Chinese Elvises, which, for Penticton, was like going to the zoo and seeing the lions and tigers in the same cage.

Anyway, after I figured I'd waited long enough, I went back out and she was still there. It was getting cold, especially for the summertime, and I snuck up right behind her.

Looks like somebody forgot about you, I said, right against the back of her neck. She screamed and everybody looked our way, then she blushed and laughed a laugh as pretty as her face when she saw everybody looking.

I don't know what happened to him, she said, and I put my arm around her and this time she didn't move. I took her into the casino and she told me all about who she was and where she was from. Allison Gibson. She was a real Penticton girl, born and raised. Her daddy owned one of the campsites by the northern lake, and her and her sister shared a room in the house he'd built there. I told her I had my own trailer, up off the highway, and she seemed to like the sound of that.

From then on we were set for each other, and I would walk down into Penticton all the time to pick her up and cruise the beach and maybe fool around behind the elementary school. After a couple of weeks she started coming up to see me at my place, and she did a good job of keeping things clean and even cooking for me a little, and I got used to having her around too.

Near the beginning of September Allison told me she'd been getting sick, and we went down to the big green Superstore in town and bought her a test. Then we went over to Wendy's and she went in the bathroom, and I got her a Spicy Chicken like she liked and waited. Sure enough, she was crying when she came out, and that sealed it. I don't think I've ever sat through a meal with so little talking. From me, at least. She just kept blubbering and saying, Donald, what are we gonna do? Like I was an almanac stuffed full of answers. I told her to stop crying and eat her food, that we would figure it all out just fine. I knew, though, that I had a decision to make, and that's why I went out to the woods with my gun that weekend.

MY OLDER BROTHER Joseph used to say that a man makes his best decisions while he's got a gun in his hand, and I thought that was some damn good advice. First off, when you got a gun, you're always the one making the decisions. Second, you can just take care of anyone who thinks you're wrong. That second reason is maybe the best one.

I started out just walking up, figuring I'd follow the curve of the mountain until I got near the top and then start back down around the other side. That would bring me out right against the highway, and from there I could hitch a ride to the park. I wasn't hunting anything particular, I was just hunting everything. I figured to take down a few birds and be happy with that, but if I caught a deer or something bigger, that would please me just fine. The important thing was to get some real thinking done.

I touched the trees as I went up, to have something more than the gun in my hands, and they felt real dry. It had barely rained that summer, except for one big storm in the middle of July, and even that had been in and out of town in one night. The grass on the mountainside was yellow and stiff, and the branches I grabbed kept snapping off in my hands. That was a bad sign, for them to be that dry, and I hoped there wouldn't be any fires before fall. There hadn't been a big one, a real burner, since I was little, but that one had been wild enough that they moved everyone out of town. Joseph used to tell me about sitting over on the other side of the lake, where everyone had camped to watch the flames and see if their houses burned. He said he remembered sitting between my mum and my dad, not being scared at all, and how everyone, the whole of Penticton out there on the beach, didn't seem worried or anything. Like they knew that if the fire took the houses they could just build them up again, and that the town was more than wood and metal sheeting.

Geoff had told me he could get me a fishing job out of Seattle, and if not in Seattle then out of somewhere on the Island. That's what Joseph left to do two years ago, right after lung cancer finished Dad, and he'd sent me letters saying nothing but good news, that you got paid well and there was no chance of waking up without there being work to do. Plus you could drink every night, if you took care of yourself, and there were lonely enough Native women at all the stops. That sounded pretty good to me. Geoff also told me he knew a guy who would give me two grand for my trailer, and I figured that was probably even more than Dad had paid for it. So things looked real good if I chose to go south for the winter, and maybe longer.

Excepting Allison. I knew what she would think about me heading down, and I was careful not to say anything about it while she was around. I had no good feelings about becoming a daddy. But she told me an abortion wasn't going to happen, that then she'd be killing her own child, our child, and there was no way, just no way, even if I paid for it. I didn't like the sound of that at all.

Punch her in the stomach, Geoff said. Geoff's a dick when it comes to treating women, but he was right, in his way. If I stayed in Penticton I'd be taking care of three by the next time I saw Elvis.

We'll be fine as long as we're together, Allison said, and as long as you love me. Now sure that sounded alright when she was in bed with her ass pressing on my legs, but in the morning it got me to worrying. Did I love her? I'd told her daddy so, when I saw him one day at the Safeway and he asked me where his daughter had been sleeping, but I was starting to feel like maybe I'd changed my mind. Geoff told me if I wanted to come down with him all I had to do was give him the word and we could have the trailer sold and a bus ticket bought within an hour.

About three quarters of the way up the mountain I came to a clearing, and figured that was as good a place as any to turn back around, even though I hadn't even fired a shot yet. I sat down to eat some cheese sandwiches Allison had packed me. They were just how I liked, no mayonnaise. It seemed funny to me that the girl could tell what I was hot for and what I wasn't, like we'd known each other since before I even thought about girls. I liked that, how being with her made me feel like I didn't have to worry about so many of the little things anymore, that she'd take care of fixing up my life. Until now. Now it seemed like I was going to have a big thing to worry about, and all the little things that went with it. A baby meant more food, more clothes, more things to weigh on my brain every time I opened my eyes in the morning. Me and Allison I liked just fine, but me and Allison and a little bundle of responsibility didn't get me excited at all. Besides, going through town I already felt my eyes getting dragged around by other women, and I knew from experience that there's no cure for restlessness.

To the west the trees got taller, then let off into a big patch of clear-cutting. There was a logging camp down at the base of that side of the mountain. Geoff and I drove there once a week to sell pot to the loggers. To the east was Penticton, squashed between the two lakes, and from it the fat grey line of highway heading out south.

A big bird, maybe a hawk, punched out of the woods just as I was polishing off my second sandwich. It flew up over my head and just hung there, like it was waiting for me to take a good shot. I unslung my rifle and braced myself against the rock, then leaned back and fired. I missed, probably by half a mile, and the recoil nearly knocked my shoulder clean out. I'm no hunter, really. All I know is point and shoot, and that it's easier to hit something when that something don't know you're coming. My dad never touched a gun in his life. But Joseph always loved coming up here and shooting, and for a while he brought me with him. He left me the rifle when he ditched town, along with the trailer. Took the truck for himself, though.

I caught a look at something pale along the treeline. I dropped down and laid myself out on the ground behind the rock. I had it pegged for a deer. That's the only thing it could be, really, or maybe a fox. For about ten minutes I lay stiller than if I was sleeping, the rock under my chin and the sun on my back. Then it came out. A cougar. I had never seen one, outside of TV. In June there had been dogs getting killed in the subdivisions down at the bottom of the mountain, and the news was full of people talking about cougars getting too brave for their own good. But no one had done anything about it, because what can you do? The city tried to throw up a bounty on skins, but the animal-rights hippies wouldn't even let them get started.

This wasn't a big fella, though. Maybe fifty feet away, but it didn't look like much more than a baby. Mountain cat. Mountain kitten, more like it.

I lay still and watched it, measuring out my breaths. It didn't seem to know where to go. Little sucker kept pawing around in circles, and then sometimes just holding still and sniffing at the air. The more it moved, the closer it came by me. After a couple of minutes it had cut the ground between us in half, easy, and I started figuring it was getting past time for me to take a shot. In fact, the more I thought about it, lying there on the ground following the thing with the end of my rifle, the more it made a damn good amount of sense.

I figured I'd let it make my big decision for me. If I can get it, I figured, that means I can head down with Geoff tomorrow. If I can't, that'll tell me I'm right for Penticton after all, and I'll stay.

I lined the little thing up. He was only twenty feet away now. I pushed the trigger down till I felt it push back.

But then I waited. I mean, I knew the good thing was to take care of Allison. For god-fearing folks, that was the only answer for what I should be doing. If I was betting against what I had pretty much figured was the decent thing, did that make me a bad person? I thought about it for a little. No. Just made me honest. What kind of man settles down to a family when he's twenty-one, with no real job and no house and no plans for how to get ahold of either? Not me, I thought. Definitely not me. The kind of dad I'd be, I was doing Allison a favour.

I squinted down the barrel and tugged the trigger in.

The first shot blew up the earth in front of him, but I don't think the kitten so much as lost a hair, and he sure didn't wait around for the second. Before I was on my feet again he was back in the trees. I took off after him. Damned if I was going to let my life get away just because I was a bad shot.

I rushed right into the trees with my gun raised and curses raining. Nothing. Spotting out a mountain cat among a couple of rocks and a patch of grass is one thing, but tracking him through the forest was going to be a real dirty handful. I moved forward, branches cutting at my face, hoping to catch another peek.

Instead I heard someone screaming. A man. Flat out hollering, like he was hurt real bad.

When I was eight my dad cut off two of his fingers sawing firewood. Joseph drove the truck to the hospital, twelve years old and barely big enough to touch the pedals, and I sat between the two of them, bawling like I was the one who'd been cut up. I had nothing on my dad, though. He was screaming like he was pumping out a baby, cursing and spitting and most of the time just plain making noise.

I shouted into the woods. The voice stopped for a minute, then shouted back. It came from farther down, and I started running toward it.

I'm coming! Keep yelling! I said, and he did, angry and awful.

What I came onto was downright primal, and it turned my feet to stone. You would've thought summer was over there was so much red. On the ground, on the trees, and all over the momma cougar and this man. I could tell from his flannel and his pants that he was a logger, but I couldn't see much more for the blood. He was kneeled over her, and it was just dripping off him like he'd showered in it. His or hers, I dunno. He looked up and saw me and let out a sound like a man saved, his mouth a black hole in a sea of red. And then he slumped forward onto her body.

That sandwich almost came right back into my mouth as I

ran over to him, but I swallowed and kept it down. The momma was dead, her throat and belly ripped right out and spread all over his shirt and his hands.

My eye, he was moaning, bitch got me in the fucking eye. It was true, his right eye was gone, and the look in the other was insane, predatory. I threw up when I saw the empty socket, couldn't hold it, but just fast and over my shoulder. Most of his right arm was gone too. There was bits of bone showing all the way from his wrist to his elbow.

Fuckin' shit, what happened to you man? I said as I got my shirt off and started tearing it into strips.

Surprised me, he said. I pushed him forward so that I could tie his head up, and I smelled that he had shit himself something fierce. Killed the bitch, he said. Fucking knifed her good.

He wasn't kidding. His knife was on the ground over by her open belly, a little fucking pocket thing. This crazy fuck had killed a cougar all by himself, even though the bitch got the jump on him. He got caught and he took care of things, no questions asked. Put his head down and ripped her throat out. I thought about the look on his face when he'd seen me, how pure crazy he had just been, bent over, ripping that little knife through her stomach over and over again, killing her a thousand times.

I thought he was passed out now, but he started screaming again when I yanked his good arm up over my shoulder.

Easy, chief, I said. Just take it easy and don't pass out and we'll get out of this all right.

I took a glance back at the momma as we headed down. Her cub had come out from wherever it had been hiding, and it went to stand by her body. We matched eyes for a second, me and the little beast, but then I slipped and had to concentrate on my footing. The sun was already setting, but I figured we would make it down before night fell. I was covered in blood, the smell of it was all over me. I'd need someone to wash me up, but after that I was going to write a note telling Allison I was gone, headed for somewhere where looking out for someone else wasn't bound to mean your life was over.

THE BASICS OF THE SPECIES

AFTER THE FIRST two weeks, Nick didn't move from in front of the television. He sat cross-legged, staring at charred corpses and rubble, wild animals and Katherine. Wrapped in a thin blanket against the cold, hair hanging before his glasses, he watched, and sometimes wept. I did my best to keep him company. On the twenty-third day she'd been gone, as I entered his apartment and was brushing the snow off my boots, he asked me if I thought he was going insane.

"Because I wouldn't know what it felt like. That's been worrying me, even more than all this bullshit with Kat. If I go crazy, I'll be the only person who doesn't know it."

"You're not going crazy, pal. This'll all be over soon," I said, and went into the kitchen with the sandwich meat I'd brought over. Inside, though, I was wondering if I'd told him the truth.

MENAGERIE MADNESS had more than 24,000 applicants. That number still boggles me, overwhelming and incomprehensible, like a phone book in full colour. Terrifying that so many people had asked to spend a month locked away, and for almost nothing. Fifty grand. There are bus drivers who get paid more. But reality TV can make you famous for being ordinary, and apparently 24,000 people liked the sound of that. I had just never imagined that Katherine would be one of them.

Neither had Nick. When she first spoke to him about it, she'd already been accepted, having made it through the interviews and screen tests. At the end of that week she'd be inside, locked away at the centre of a televised panopticon. She'd told him she was doing it, and he asked what would happen to their relationship. They'd been dating for a little more than a year, but apparently that meant a lot more to him than to her. She said it would be a test; she wanted to see if what they had could withstand some separation. He said he didn't need a test, he just needed her. She said that was nice, and very sweet, but that her mind was made up. And that was the end of the discussion.

THE FIRST SHOW was, in many ways, the worst. Before it aired, we had only our imaginations to draw on, and we couldn't conceive of anything too terrible. At least, I couldn't. Nick, I'm sure, pictured Katherine and a room full of sweaty Chippendales, all having their way with her in any number of lurid positions. But we could only worry about what he thought might happen, once the show began, Nick was able to cast the parts in all his nightmares.

Nick lived out in Scarborough, in an apartment building that grew out of a strip mall. He could have done better. In high school he was always at the top of our class, and even though his parents kicked him out the day after graduation, his marks got him accepted by York on a full ride. But he coasted through that and into a job writing code for office e-mail filters, ensuring your boss found out right away if you wrote a dirty note to the receptionist. The work didn't dumb his intellect, just wasted it.

November was promising a bad winter; it had been snowing for days, and the cautious pace of the traffic made me late. Nick had melted cheese onto some nachos, and he pushed them forward as I sat down on his Salvation Army sofa.

"You barely made it," he said. He had just got out of the shower, and there was a piece of toilet paper stuck to his cheek where he'd cut himself shaving. He was dressed up, too, wearing a blue button-down and khakis. Like he was going out on a date.

The Monkees-esque singalong theme music played over a rapid montage of each housemate. They fit the archetypes pretty well. An obviously gay East Indian guy, Marcus, was like the reality show double play. Jerome, from Quebec, was a frail, artsy-looking thirtysomething, sporting a heavy peacoat with the collar turned up toward his wispy goatee. Sarah, an innocent-looking Chinese girl, smiled shyly against a backdrop of the Rockies. Then Jamie, an all-Canadian Vancouver boy with a wrinkled rugby jersey and a toothy smile. And finally our Katherine, wearing a pink scarf over a denim jacket and pushing her lips forward in a pout. They had done something with her hair, swept it up and piled it on top of her head, and it made her look like she'd spent her whole life in front of the camera.

"She's the hot one," Nick said. "They cast her as the hot one." Her looks were not a surprise, we just hadn't realized how well they would translate to the small screen.

"Congratulations."

"Yeah, thanks." He pulled his legs up to sit cross-legged on his armchair.

Alistair, the host, looking every bit as greasy as his former-prime-minister father, bounded into the room where the castmates had gathered. For some reason, a black band encircled the left arm of his suit.

He made all the introductions, and as Katherine shook Jamie's hand the camera zoomed in on the men's faces leering down her top. A cutaway to Jamie alone showed him speaking to the camera.

"I didn't know one of the animals was going to be a fox," he said. I groaned.

"Fucker," Nick said.

Alistair toured them around the house. The two girls would sleep in one room, the guys in another. There was a shared kitchen, a den full of couches and futons, and a wall that opened onto the "reserve," the area where all the animals were meant to stay. Off the den was a "confession room," about the size of a walk-in closet, which housed a camera and another couch.

"It's here in the confession room where you can tell Canada your secrets," he said, pausing to give the camera an exaggerated wink. "And now ... let me introduce you to the rest of the house-guests." He waved his hand, and the wall off the den rose up like a garage door.

Nick spat Coke across the coffee table. A penguin and a wolver-ine stood side by side with a chimpanzee and something that looked like a cross between a horse and a dog. Together, they resembled a kind of evolutionary prison lineup. They were held back by trainers, but as they came fully into view these khaki-clad crew members scampered offscreen, and the animals quickly broke ranks — the penguin tottered forward aimlessly, the chimp jumped onto the couch where Jerome was lounging, the horse-dog looked around in bewilderment, and the wolverine simply collapsed to the floor and closed its eyes, unimpressed and exhausted.

"You're kidding me," I said. Alistair was introducing the animals, kneeling cautiously beside the wolverine. "Greenpeace or whoever are going to be all over them."

"I bet the animals will get treated better than the humans," Nick said. The horse-dog, we learned, was something called an okapi, and the penguin was the oldest male Emperor in captivity, so they called him Grandpa. Bantam, the wolverine, was nearly blind, and had been slated for euthanasia until the show's producers "rescued" him. The chimpanzee was named Mr. Chuckles.

"Katherine won't be able to stand this," Nick said. "She hates monkeys; they scare the shit out of her." This detail hadn't escaped the production crew, and the camera cut to Katherine's horrified face. She had drawn her legs up onto the couch and held a hand over her mouth. As if on cue, the chimp crawled on the French guy and shat in his lap.

"And it looks like Jerome has met Mr. Chuckles," Alistair said with a straight face; that impressed me. "I know you're all going to have a wonderful time together, here on ..." Again he paused to look directly into the camera, giving the entire thing a Vaudevillian air, "... *Menagerie Madness!*"

FOR THE FIRST few days I watched casually, but Nick was hooked right away, and soon I also became fascinated by Katherine and her new group of friends. We looked on as they tried to feed Grandpa or ride poor Wumpus, the okapi, who grew more pathetic by the day.

For a while, it seemed as though we were the only ones paying attention. No one else talked about the show at work, which I could kind of understand, since there really wasn't much drama. The housemates got on well together, despite their diverse backgrounds, and their conversations were almost always adventures in tedium. The animals were practically a nonfactor. Katherine quickly outgrew her fear of Mr. Chuckles, and spent more time dodging the increasingly lecherous Jamie. Alistair's black arm band, we came to learn, was in commemoration of the show's initial host, who had unfortunately gotten caught examining the wrong end of a llama during pre-taping. The llama, apparently, didn't share his feelings, and ended up kicking the guy to death. In interviews Alistair referred to the incident as "our great tragedy."

After a week, when the time for the first vote came, Sarah the Asian girl was unceremoniously booted off. The viewers eliminated her by an incredible margin. She had spent most of her time making sketches on a giant notepad, which she refused to reveal to anyone. Later, when this pad was investigated, the audience saw that it contained bizarre, oversized caricatures of the other housemates. Critics would eventually praise these pieces as the advent of "reality art," and the pages sold one by one on eBay for a total that reached millions. But that was much later, after the show broke all viewing records and became the twisted centre of everything.

IT WAS THE DAY after Sarah left that the Toronto attacks happened, and the world turned upside down. We all got trapped in some crazy snowglobe, shaken in ways we never saw coming. I was driving and there was a Tragically Hip song playing, "Little Bones." The announcer cut it off, saying something about the Toronto-Dominion Centre towers. But she was talking too fast, almost babbling, and I pulled over because it scared me that someone on the radio should sound like they were crying. My first thought was that I wouldn't have to go to work, that no one would, and later, watching the coverage, I remembered this and was embarrassed.

GRAINY AMATEUR footage showed flames bursting from doorways and windows. Tiny human silhouettes were visible through clouds of debris and ash, limbs contorted into sickening, unnatural poses. The shot that was replayed over and over showed a young girl whose body had been blown off at the stomach. A sheet lay over her exposed chest, and the viewer's attention was brought to her face, eyes closed, entirely at peace. A single track of blood ran down her cheek, so that it appeared as if she was weeping even in death.

Aerial views of the city were clouded by dust, and information was slow to leak out. The death toll after the first day reached over a thousand, and those were just the easily counted bodies that lined the streets and gutters. No one seemed brave enough to estimate how many more remained trapped within the rubble. I somehow went to sleep that night, the grim voices of politicians and news anchors looping endlessly through my head.

THE TERRORISTS weren't Islamic, as many had first expected. It appeared they weren't anything, just terrorists in the purest sense of the word. No group claimed responsibility. Security tapes showed the attackers dressed in black trench coats and fedoras, walking calmly into their targets, the bombs in duffel bags by their sides. Adolescent web pages celebrating their nihilism sprang up almost immediately.

Around noon I found my way to Nick's. Toronto was suddenly barren. Although people had been discouraged from evacuating, the morning news showed an infinite assembly line clogging every highway out of the city. I didn't even consider leaving.

Unmarked police cars roared along the street, sirens flashing but silent. I left my cellphone on my kitchen counter; its network had collapsed sometime shortly after the first bomb.

Nick was dressed in a terry-cloth bathrobe, and it didn't look like he had slept. His kitchen was littered with unwashed dishes. He opened the door and then went immediately back to his chair.

"They haven't told them," he said.

"What?"

"They haven't told them. Inside the house, they don't know."

"You're kidding." I sat down. He had on the *Menagerie* channel, and it was true. Katherine was napping beside Bantam, and the three guys sat in a circle with Mr. Chuckles, trying to teach him how to high five. The penguin was sometimes visible in the corner of the screen, flopping around in an oversized baby pool. Wumpus was nowhere to be seen.

"It's amazing," Nick said. "Total ignorance. I'm kind of jealous. Nothing can go wrong in that little world, they're so protected."

"Yeah," I said, "but ..."

"What?"

"But it's not right."

Nick reached a hand inside his bathrobe and scratched himself.

"Have you heard from Tyler?" he said. Tyler Bigam was a guy we'd known in high school. He worked for a currency trading firm in one of the six towers.

"Not yet. I sent him an e-mail. Don't have a phone number."

"He worked high up," Nick said. "I can't see how ..." He raised his eyebrows.

"Yeah."

I sat and we watched in silence, happy to escape to their alternate universe. At exactly one o'clock, a bell rang throughout the house and Alistair entered through the giant, barred front door. He was wearing a black suit, a white shirt and a black tie — funeral attire. He had everyone sit down in the living room and face him.

"I have something very grave to tell you," Alistair said. Katherine, who was still drowsy from her nap, was rubbing at her eyes. "I don't want you to get scared." He paused, perhaps expecting some greater reaction, but they all just gazed dumbly at him.

"Yesterday, there was a major disaster here in Toronto. I can't tell you exactly what, only that it was an event that will surely go down in history as a dark, dark day for our city, and for Canada."

"You are kidding," Jerome said.

"This is no joking matter, I assure you," Alistair said.

Jerome gave him a disgusted look.

"But you won't tell us what it was?" he said.

"No." Alistair spread his hands out before him. "I can't. The rules of the game stipulate that you must remain isolated. However, I can offer you the option of leaving at this time, should you so desire."

"That's ridiculous," Marcus said.

At the mention of the possibility of an early exit, Nick sat up straight.

"They're making it into a fucking event," he said. "It's disgusting." But he didn't even look toward the remote.

"What if something happened to someone we know?" Katherine said. "Would you tell us that? Are our families safe?"

"Of course," Alistair said. "Although, you have to understand ... it's impossible for us to know everything. There may be people to whom you are connected that we're not aware of."

"What if we all leave?" Jerome said. "If we all go, you have no show. You know that, right?" His French accent had that natural tone of disdain. "If we all say we go, then the show would end, and so we can force you to tell us." He looked around at the others, seeking some support, but they kept their heads down.

"That's a chance the producers are prepared to take," Alistair said quickly, obviously prepared for such a question. The four eyed one another, measuring their chances. No one seemed willing to speak first.

"I'll go," Marcus finally said. He stood up. "I can't stay here for another three weeks if they're hiding the apocalypse out there." Jerome sighed, then cleared his throat in disgust.

"*Moi aussi*," he said, scratching at his goatee. "I think it is bullshit, but I cannot go on without knowing."

"Jamie? Katherine?" Alistair said. Jamie was staring at the floor and shaking his head.

"I need that fifty grand," he said. "I'm in, fuck it."

"Me too," Katherine said. I glanced over at Nick, but he didn't say anything. I saw a tendon flex in his neck as he clenched his jaw.

"Alright," Alistair said. "Jerome and Marcus, please come with me. Jamie and Katherine, congratulations. One of you is fifty-thousand dollars richer. We'll find out who in three weeks." He got up and walked back toward the entry door, Jerome and Marcus in his wake. As he began to close it, he looked up at Katherine and Jamie.

"I'm sorry," he said. "And good luck."

Jamie stood up and walked to the door, trying the handle. It didn't move. He turned to Katherine.

"Me and you, babe," he said.

"Yeah," she said, running a hand through her hair. "You got it." She stood up, went into her room, and lay down on the bed.

Nick sunk deep into his seat.

"Can you believe that?" he said. "She's not coming out. That's how much the money means to her."

"But she doesn't know," I said. "She has no idea of what's going on out here. I can't believe they're not cancelling the show."

"Of course they're not," Nick said. "This show will be more

popular than ever. People will need this, it's the ultimate escape. I bet the ratings soar, man." Of course, he ended up being right. By choosing to ignore the attacks, Katherine and Jamie became their symbol.

"But that's your girlfriend in there. Not a 'they,' man. Katherine. And she's locked away while her city is falling apart." We sat for a moment, staring at the tiny figures on screen, and then Nick turned off the set. Very quietly, he asked if I wanted to go to the zoo.

EVEN IF IT hadn't been the day after the attacks, the zoo still would have been empty because of the cold. The walkways hadn't been shovelled, and we had to pound holes for our feet as we struggled from cage to cage. Many of the animals had been taken away for the winter, I guess to warmer climates, or perhaps just indoors somewhere. I had been surprised the place was even open.

"Two dollars," said the spherical woman at the kiosk. She kept her eyes on us as she tore the first two tickets of the day from her roll.

Only the Canadian Tundra section remained fully stocked, the more worldly animals simply weren't hardy enough. We watched a herd of maybe a half-dozen elk in silence. Nick fished some quarters out of his pocket and bought a handful of brown pellets in an attempt to feed the things, but they kept their distance from the bars, refusing to acknowledge us.

We passed some Arctic wolves that rushed up and bared their fangs as we approached.

"I thought wolves were passive." Their fur was thin and patchy; some looked almost as if they had been sheared.

"I don't think they've been fed in a while," Nick said. He offered some brown pellets to a large male that had pressed itself against the bars. It snapped at him and barked. Two smaller females sat back on their haunches and began to howl. The others quickly gathered around them and joined in, creating a loud, mournful wail.

"The zookeeper must know what he's doing," I said.

"Yeah," Nick said again. He was reading a sign that described the basics of the species. "They mate for life, did you know that?"

"That's nice," I said. I did notice that each male had drawn close to a specific female, and that all the pairs were howling in unison.

"Do you think they love each other?" Nick said.

"I don't know. It looks like it. Yeah, sure, they love each other. Don't you think wolves can love?"

"They're mammals," he said. "Just like us. Built to sleep and eat and fuck. Love means believing someone is better than that. Suspending reality for them, or hoping they will for you."

"So?"

"So, yeah. I mean, they don't look too happy, but they're still watching after each other. That seems like love to me."

THE REDUCED CAST meant that either Jamie or Katherine was always in focus, and that they were forced to spend all their time together. Their conversations began to acquire new depth, and they had every first-date conversation imaginable — the siblings, the parents, the jobs, the hobbies. These framed the more somber conversations they would have late in the evening about what might have happened, what they were missing. Smoke blocked out the sky above the reserve for several days after the attacks, throwing an apocalyptic pall over the house. They huddled together in the doorway to stare at it, and wondered about aliens and al Qaeda, earthquakes and endings. The animals sensed something was wrong. The penguin was the worst — he stood stone still for days, facing the corner of the compound and shaking like his flipper was stuck in a socket. Bantam took it hard too, growing skittish and uneasy, tearing at the furniture.

And then Jamie and Katherine began to flirt, with a kind of high-school wariness that I'm sure the audience at large found endearing. They became engaged in a perpetual tickle fight, and were suddenly incapable of walking by one another without a poke in the back or between the ribs. I watched snippets of this from my own place, but I still found myself at Nick's fairly often. It was around that time that he asked me if I thought he was going crazy. I spoke to him from the kitchen as I prepared a sandwich.

"Did you see the latest numbers?" Every morning brought another horror story as entire floors of some buildings were dragged from the wreckage. Tyler was found on the second day, alongside the receptionist from his office. The phone system was still unreliable, and we found out through another friend of ours, Cheryl Wasserman, who had taken it upon herself to visit everyone who might have been worried about Ty.

"By the way," she said to Nick as she stood at the door of the apartment, "I've been watching Katherine on TV. I really think she's doing great."

"Thanks," Nick said.

"But that guy is a total creep," she added. Nick nodded.

"Total," he said.

We watched as the lootings began, and officials became torn between trying to rescue potential survivors and halt the razing of Toronto. Supermarkets were emptied within hours, and, overnight, people began boarding up their homes. In Forest Hill, where the inhabitants had long since fled, the mobs rolled in through windows and garage doors, hauling out dining-room sets and stainless steel refrigerators. Banks and stores remained closed near the downtown core, and after my car ran out of gas I had to walk between Nick's apartment and my own. Stations in our neighborhood were still open, but prices had jumped to nearly ten dollars a litre. I made the walk with a hammer in one hand and steak knife in the other, just in case. The army had been called in, we heard, but they seemed to be taking their time showing up. All fourteen of them.

"I don't care about this anymore," Nick said. He switched the channel from the news coverage, where a helicopter circled a burning Tim Hortons, and found the show. "I've reached my caring limit, you know? I want it to be someone else's problem."

Katherine and Jamie were sitting on the couch. Mr. Chuckles lay between them, and Katherine was idly rubbing the creature's belly. In honour of the show's halfway point, they enjoyed a five-course French meal, eating at the coffee table. Katherine fed most of her entrée, a piece of venison, to Bantam.

"Tell me about your boyfriend," Jamie said.

"They've mentioned you?" I said.

"Yeah," Nick said. "Yesterday sometime, he asked her if she was seeing anyone outside, and she said yeah, but that was it. Didn't say my name or anything."

"He's not my boyfriend," Katherine said. "He's ... I don't know, we've been very close for a long time, you know? He's important to me, let's say that."

"Gotcha," Jamie said. "I know exactly what you mean."

"But I'm glad we did this. I'm glad I came on here," Katherine said. "I think I've learned a lot about myself in the past two weeks."

"Like what?" Jamie said. He was staring at her with big, blank blue eyes. I could imagine him running the same game in a dark bar, throwing question after question at a girl in an effort to make her feel important. Katherine was drumming her fingers on Mr. Chuckles' stomach.

"Like ... I think how I've gotten to know you, over the past few days ... when you're in a relationship you forget very quickly what it's like to meet other people. I don't mean date, just ... you stop making new friends, you know?"

"Definitely," Jamie said. He had been edging closer to her on the couch, and as he ran into the space where Mr. Chuckles was sprawled he leaned over and lifted the monkey into his lap. "I think this whole thing has really been a good experiment so far. When you're so alone, you really get a chance to explore yourself."

"That's exactly what I mean," Katherine said. Then, suddenly, Jamie made his move, leaning forward and putting a hand behind her head, pulling her lips to his. She resisted, for a moment, and then gave in, and Mr. Chuckles scampered away screaming.

"Turn it off," I said. But Nick didn't answer. His mouth hung open, and when I went for the remote he wordlessly picked it up and moved it away from my reach. So we watched as they tore each others' clothes off, and Katherine pulled her hands down Jamie's body, along his collarbone and ribs, dragging over each like they were the edges of cliffs. When she got to his belt buckle I stood, walked over to the TV, and turned it off.

"What the fuck?" Nick cried. His voice was strained, and I could see his eyes were watering.

"What the fuck? You want to watch that? She's your girl-friend, man! You want to torture yourself like that? I don't ... Jesus, Nick!" He grabbed the remote and threw it at me, missing badly.

"You got it, she's my girlfriend," he yelled. "If she wants to fuck us up, that's fine, but I deserve to see it."

"Why would you want to watch that?"

He put his head down for a second, then reared up out of his seat toward me, getting right in my face.

"Why are you here?" he said in a whisper. His breath was terrible, I could tell he hadn't brushed his teeth in a long time. "Why do you want to watch me go through this, huh? Why do you want to watch?"

I didn't say anything, and backed toward the door.

"Why can't you just leave me alone?" he said. "You've been having fun, coming over here. It's easy for you, you're removed from the situation. You're watching my car crash, and you're loving it."

"What are you talking about, man? I'm your friend, I'm trying to help."

"You want to help?" Tears were streaming down his face. "You can help by getting the fuck out, buddy."

I was at the door, and I shook my head at him as I kicked my shoes on.

"Thank you," he said, and slammed it behind me.

IT WAS THROUGH me that Nick had met Katherine. She and I had worked together at a securities firm — she was a receptionist there when I began doing my associate work. We hit it off immediately. There was an energy to her that I always marvelled at, an exuberance that I'd never encountered in anyone before. At the company Christmas party we ended up in the same elevator after more than a few trips to the open bar, and before long we were fumbling with each other's buckles and snaps against the door of the hotel room I'd rented. For a few hours, we couldn't contain ourselves. The sex was almost angry, and I was far more aggressive than I'd ever been with anyone else. The next morning, though, as the light finally began to filter through the window, awkwardness crept over us. We made a pact not to discuss what had happened with anyone, and a few weeks later I introduced her to Nick.

AFTER HE KICKED me out we didn't speak for a week. That's when it became impossible to avoid the show. Katherine's picture was suddenly appearing on the front page beside coverage of the downtown unrest, her face sitting eerily beside photos of looters in handcuffs and sobbing rescue workers. An old hippie editorialist named Oswald Sebastian had begun writing about how the show represented a lost fragment of the city's innocence, and how Katherine and Jamie should be kept inside forever, supported and maintained like some kind of museum exhibit.

Of course, any idea of innocence was shattered by the ads the networks had begun running: montages of various humping animals — rhinos, poodles, beetles — between shots of Katherine and Jamie's own barely concealed fucking. *Menagerie Madness*, read text scrolling across the screen, *Where the Wild Things Are*.

ON THE MORNING of their last day in confinement, Bantam attacked Jamie. It happened innocently enough: Jamie had awoken early, and stumbled into the kitchen to make coffee. Bantam was curled up by the space heater that had been installed by the fridge, and Jamie, still groggy from sleep and not seeing the little beast, stepped on his tail. As he looked down, Bantam leapt at him, swatting his face with one clawed paw. The gesture was clearly more defensive than predatory, and the endless replays that morning only enforced this. Almost before Jamie hit the ground, a team of handlers rushed into the compound, grabbing Bantam by the jaw and dragging him off screen. Two paramedics emerged to help Jamie, who had really only suffered some scratches on his face. To his credit, he bore it stoically.

"Guy came out of nowhere," he said, touching the wound and then starting in confusion at the blood on his hand. The paramedics stitched him up wordlessly.

"What happened, what happened?" Katherine ran into the room in pajama pants and a T-shirt, hugging herself against the cold.

"Hey babe," Jamie said. "I pissed off Bantam, I think."

"Oh my god," she said. "Are you alright? Did he get you anywhere else?"

"No, no, I'm fine," Jamie said. He looked toward the reserve, where the trainers had vanished with the wolverine. "I just hope Bantam's okay."

"He'll be fine," Katherine said, sniffing in dismissal. She ran some water onto a cloth and used it to clean the remaining blood from Jamie's face.

My phone, only recently restored to service, began to ring. It was Nick.

"Did you see that?" he said.

"Yeah, just watched it."

"Unbelievable. I thought it was going to tear him apart."

"Yeah. It's a good thing it's their last day, I think Bantam might get some hard feelings. Nobody likes getting their tail stepped on." Nick laughed.

"No, I guess they don't."

I didn't reply, and the line was silent for a second.

"Are you going to come by tonight?" Nick said.

"Should I?"

"Yeah, I'd like to watch the end with you. I mean ... I'm sorry about the other day. I've been doing better. I figure there are millions of guys getting cheated on right now."

"Yeah," I said. "But not on national television, man. Not in front of the whole fucking world."

"Yeah," he said. "That's true."

NICK MET ME at the door. His face had become a jumble of sharp angles that stuck out against his hollow cheeks, and his eyes were bloodshot and watery. They darted around like hyperactive toddlers, sweeping the room and then turning to the floor.

"They caught the terrorists," he said.

"What?" I had brought over a bottle of champagne, thinking he'd appreciate the irony, and I set it down just inside the door as I followed him into the living room.

"The towers." Nick led me to the TV. "They caught the guys who did it. Found them all together in some hotel in Quebec City, strung out on heroin and almost ready to kill each other. I guess they'd locked themselves in there since it happened. They all got scared one of them was going to go to the cops. They're just kids, man."

He was right. They looked barely old enough to drink. There were images of plainclothes RCMP officers, dragging four of them across the tarmac, bags over their heads. But the bags were ripped off as the four were hauled up a set of stairs onto a waiting plane, and the lens tightened until their faces filled the screen. They were all white, and disturbingly young — not much more than teenagers. One was mildly overweight, and you could see tears in his eyes. All of them seemed so small, so pathetic. Nick switched to the show. Jamie and Katherine were packing their things, and hardly speaking to each other.

"Doesn't look like the two of them are ready for life together in the real world, does it?" I said.

Nick nodded. His phone lay on the table, unplugged, and I pointed at it.

"Reporters," he said. "Around two days ago they started calling. Everyone wants the interview with Katherine's 'other man.'"

"You're kidding."

"You think it's funny?" He pointed at the window. "They were camped out in the street last night, trying to film into here. They left this morning, I guess to go to the site to get coverage of the big moment, the exit into the real world or whatever." He kneaded his temples. "Did you vote?" The polls had been open for twenty-four hours.

"No, forgot," I said. "Did you?"

"Yeah." There was a sheepish tone to his admission.

"For who?"

"Katherine."

I looked at him and raised an eyebrow.

"Fuck," he said, shrugging in apology. "I'm not going to let him have it!" I laughed. I couldn't tell if he had come to terms with it or not.

Nick seemed very stable, but he looked anything but. I wondered if he had accepted how it was no longer about Katherine, because she was gone, there was no question about it. Women turn that point in relationships and there's no bringing them back; you go instantly from being Prince Charming to Quasimodo, and no spell will reverse the transformation. Nick seemed to have reached an understanding of this, but his appearance seemed so tattered that I wondered if he was pretending for me.

Still, I felt glad to be there. Through the little window by his seat I could see that it had begun to snow again.

I HEATED UP some canned soup as the voting drew to a close, and over New England clam chowder we watched Alistair sit the two of them down in what had become a familiar position, facing him on the couch. The other furniture had been removed from the room, and blown-up photos of Katherine, Jamie and the animals hung from the walls.

"This is it," Alistair said, pulling a small white envelope from the pocket of his jacket. "A month of your lives has been devoted to this house, and to these animals." He gestured toward Wumpus, who was stumbling over and over again into the glass of a sliding door.

"It's been awesome," Jamie said.

"You've both certainly shared something," Alistair said. "However, whether you want to share this envelope is a decision one of you will have to make alone. Inside is a cheque for fifty thousand dollars, and there's only one name on it."

"So open it," Katherine said. She had her arms crossed across her chest, and seemed oddly perturbed by Alistair's presence. I couldn't tell if she wanted to stay or couldn't wait to leave.

"Of course," Alistair said. He struggled with the envelope for a moment, and finally tore it in half to get at the message inside. He read it and looked up.

"I'm very proud of you two," he said. "It took great bravery to remain here."

They were both silent.

"Jamie," Alistair said. "Congratulations."

Jamie leapt off the couch and onto the coffee table, pumping his fist in the air. He was screaming, but nothing that could be described as words. Just simple, extremely loud exhortations of satisfaction.

"Wow," I said.

"Yeah," Nick said. "Looks like the little girl votes will always carry the day, huh?" We had figured this would be the largest demographic, and that it would unsurprisingly favour Jamie.

"Yeah," I said.

Alistair jumped to Katherine's couch, and leaned over to her as Jamie continued to dance around the room.

"Do you think Jamie will share the winnings with you, Katherine?"

Jamie abruptly stopped his victory dance. Katherine looked at him as if he was once again a stranger to her. After a moment, she turned back to Alistair.

"No," she said. She wasn't audibly crying, but the camera zoomed in close enough that tears could be seen making tracks down her cheeks.

"We made a pact," Jamie said, coming back to sit down on the couch. "I'm going to keep it all. It was up to the audience to decide, and they've decided it." It was apparent that he was having trouble containing his excitement.

"So how do you feel, Katherine?" Alistair said.

She looked right at the camera.

"I just can't wait to get home," she said. "I miss the people I love. I miss being taken care of. It's been great, but I'm finished. I know people are waiting for me."

Nick sat back in his chair and sighed.

"That bitch," he said, almost under his breath.

"And now," Alistair said, his voice darkening, "it is with utmost gravity that I must inform you about what you've missed. While you have laughed and played, the world has been in mourning." He was cut off by Nick, who stood up suddenly and grabbed his tiny television from the underside. He yanked it from its stand with a roar. The weight of it seemed to be more than he expected, and he swung, trying to maintain his balance and avoid falling with it on top of him. He took three steps, pirouetting and swaying against the wall, and then tottered to the window. I watched as he pulled it open and gave the set a shove, rocking it forward and out. He leaned to watch it fall, desperate to witness every second of its three-storey descent.

I lunged forward just in time to see it explode, the crack of the casing drowning out the tinkle of the shattered display. A pyramid of black trash bags towered against his building. They were stuffed full, splitting at their sides. Nick's TV had fallen beside them, into a landscape of leaking garbage. Looking down at the deserted street, I realized that we had all been living in squalor for some time now.

ACKNOWLEDGEMENTS

GREAT THANKS to those publications in whose pages versions of these stories were previously published, including *THIS Magazine* ("Home Movies," "Such Sights to Show You"), *EXILE Literary Quarterly* ("Indigenous Beasts") and the *Nassau Weekly*. Also thanks to the Princeton University Creative Writing Department, Lynn Henry and Martha Sharpe, all of whom helped greatly in the creation and development of this collection. Finally, a debt is owed to Junot Diaz. "The Helmet" is written after his own "Ysrael."

By printing INDIGENOUS BEASTS on paper made from 100% post-consumer recycled fibre rather than virgin tree fibre, Raincoast Books has made the following ecological savings:

- 30 trees
- 1,195 kilograms of greenhouse gases (equivalent to driving an average North American car for 3 months)
- 21 million BTUs (equivalent to the power consumption of a North American home over 3 months)
- 41,404 litres of water
- 637 kilograms of solid waste

RAINCOAST BOOKS
www.raincoast.com

ANCIENT FOREST
FRIENDLY